Carol Marinelli recently filled in a form where she was asked for her job title and was thrilled, after all these years, to be able to put down her answer as 'writer'. Then it asked what Carol did for relaxation and, after chewing her pen for a moment, Carol put down the truth—'writing'. The third question asked, 'What are your hobbies?' Well, not wanting to look obsessed or, worse still, boring, she crossed the fingers on her free hand and answered 'swimming and tennis'. But, given that the chlorine in the pool does terrible things to her highlights, and the closest she's got to a tennis racket in the last couple of years is watching the Australian Open, I'm sure you can guess the real answer!

Recent titles by the same author:

BEHOLDEN TO THE THRONE*
BANISHED TO THE HAREM*
AN INDECENT PROPOSITION
A SHAMEFUL CONSEQUENCE
 (Empire of the Sands)

*linked titles

Did you know these are also available as eBooks?
Visit www.millsandboon.co.uk

'Santo...' As soon as she opened the door Ella regretted it.

There were some things she simply shouldn't see, and immediately Ella knew why he hadn't answered her.

The length of Santo's body was covered by bubbles and his head rested on the edge of the bath. His eyes were screwed closed, his lips were pressed together, and for once Ella wasn't catching her boss doing something inappropriate. *That* she could deal with. What she couldn't immediately deal with was the fact that Santo Corretti—a man who charmed his way through life, who always had a smart answer for everything, who she was sure cared about nothing but movies and getting laid—was lying in a bath unshaven, with bruises on his chest, looking battered. But not just physically—he looked broken.

She had at times wondered if there were any feelings to be had in that beautiful head, but now he lay there, clearly shattered, and she watched as he blew out a breath and the mask returned.

SICILY'S CORRETTI DYNASTY

The more powerful the family...the darker the secrets!
Introducing the Correttis; Sicily's most scandalous family!
Behind the closed doors of their opulent palazzo, ruthless
desire and the lethal Coretti charm are alive and well.

We invite you to step over the threshold
and enter the Correttis' dark and dazzling world...

The Empire

Young, rich and notoriously handsome, the Correttis'
legendary exploits regularly feature in Sicily's tabloid pages!

The Scandal

But how long can their reputations withstand the glaring heat
of the spotlight before their family's secrets are exposed?

The Legacy

Once nearly destroyed by the secrets cloaking their thirst
for power, the new generation of Correttis are riding high
again—and no disgrace or scandal will stand in their way...

Sicily's Corretti Dynasty

8 volumes to collect—you won't want to miss out!

A LEGACY
OF SECRETS

BY
CAROL MARINELLI

© Harlequin Books S.A. 2013

Special thanks and acknowledgement are given to Carol Marinelli
for her contribution to the *Sicily's Corretti Dynasty* series.

ISBN: 978 0 263 23470 1

PROLOGUE

'Please.'

Ella wasn't sure how many times that word had been said to her in the past, but she knew that she would forever recall this time.

'Please, Ella, don't go.'

She stood at the departure terminal of the busy Sydney International Airport, passport and boarding pass in hand, and looked into her mother's pleading eyes—the same amber eyes as her own—and she almost relented. How could she possibly leave her to deal with her father alone?

But, given all that had happened, how could she stay?

'You have a beautiful home....'

'No!' Ella would not be swayed. 'I have a flat that I bought in the hope that you would move in with me. I thought that you'd finally decide to leave him, and yet you won't.'

'I can't.'

'You can.' Ella stood firm. 'I have done everything to help you leave and yet you still refuse.'

'He's my husband.'

'And I'm your daughter.' Ella's eyes flashed with suppressed anger. 'He beat me, Mum!'

'Because you upset him. Because you try to get me to leave…' Her mother had been in Australia for more than thirty years, was married to an Australian, and yet her English was still poor. Ella knew that she could stand here and argue her point some more, but there wasn't time for that. Instead she said the words she had planned to say and gave her mother one final chance to leave. 'Come with me.'

Then Ella handed her mother the ticket she had secretly purchased.

'How?'

'I've brought your passport with me.' Ella pulled it out of her bag and handed it to her mother to show that she was serious and that she really had thought this through. 'You can walk away now, Mum. You can go back to Sicily and be with your sisters. You can have a life.…' She saw her mother wrestle with the decision. She missed her country so much, spoke about her sisters all the time, and if she would just have the courage to walk away then Ella would help her in any way that she could.

'I can't.'

There was simply no point, but Ella did her best to persuade her mum. Right up to check-in, right up to the departure gate, Ella tried to convince her mother to leave, but she had decided now that the subject was closed.

'Have a nice trip, Ella.'

'I'm not going for a holiday, Mum,' Ella said. She wanted her mother to realise how serious this was, that she wasn't just going to be away for a few weeks. 'I'm going there to look for work.'

'But you said you will visit Sicily.'

'I might.' Ella honestly didn't know. 'I don't know if I can, Mum. I'd hoped to go there with you. I think I'll stay in Rome.'

'Well, if you do get to Sicily, give my love to your aunts. Tell them…' Gabriella faltered for a moment.

'*Don't* tell them, you mean.' Ella looked at her mum, who would be in trouble for even coming to the airport, and couldn't believe she was expecting Ella to tell her aunts how fantastic her life was in Australia, to keep up the pretence. 'Are you asking me to lie?'

'Why you do this to me?' Gabriella demanded, as she did whenever Ella didn't conform or questioned things. Possibly Ella was more Sicilian than she gave herself credit for, because as her mother used the very familiar line, Ella was tempted to use it herself. *Why you do this to me? Why did you stand and scream as you watched your daughter being beaten? Why didn't you have the guts to get up and leave?* Of course she didn't say that. Ella hadn't shared her feelings with anyone, not even her mum, since that day.

'I have to go, Mum.' Ella looked up at the board— she really did have to, customs would take forever—but at the last moment her voice cracked. 'Mum, please…'

'Ella, go.'

Gabriella wept as she said goodbye but Ella didn't— she hadn't since that terrible day two months ago. Instead she hugged her mum and headed through customs and then sat dry-eyed on the plane with an empty seat beside her, nursing her guilt for leaving her mother behind, but knowing deep down there was nothing more she could do.

She was twenty-seven years old, and had spent enough of her life trying to get her mother away from her father. Even her job had been chosen with money, rather than passion, in mind.

Ella had worked as a junior assistant for a couple of CEOs, then moved through the ranks, eventually becoming a PA to a politician. She'd spent the past two years in Canberra, dreading what she might come home to in Sydney.

Unable to live like that, she had swapped a very good job for a not-so-good one, and bought a home nearer her parents. Now, after all those years of trying to help her mum, Ella knew she just had to get away.

She had references in her bag and could speak Italian.

It was time to get a life.

Her life.

It never entered her head that she might need some time off to heal from all she had endured—instead Ella's focus was on finding work.

Except it was just rather more intimidating than she'd first thought.

It was January, and she had left the hot Australian summer for a cold Italian winter. Rome was busier than anywhere Ella had ever been. The Gypsies seemed to make a beeline for her every time she ventured from the hotel, but she took in the sites, stood in awe in the Vatican and threw a coin in the Trevi Fountain, as her mother had told her to do. But what was the point, Ella thought, for her mother would never be back.

She took a train to Ostia Antica, visited the ruins and froze as she walked along the beach, wondering when the healing would start, when the revelation that she had done the right thing by leaving would strike.

It didn't.

So instead of sitting around waiting, Ella set about looking for work.

'You have a lot of experience for someone your age, but...' It was the same wherever she went—yes, her résumé was impressive, but even though they were conversing in Italian, Claudia explained at her interview, as the others had yesterday, Ella's Italian simply wasn't good enough for the agency to put her forward to any of the employers on their books.

'You understand it better than you speak it,' Claudia said. She really had been nice, so Ella chose not to be offended. 'Is there any other type of work you are interested in?'

Ella was about to say no, to shake her head, but with nothing to lose she was honest. 'The film industry.'

'We don't handle actors.'

'No, no...' Ella shook her head. 'I'm interested in directing.' It was all she had ever wanted to do, but saving up enough money to give her mother the option to move had been her priority. Instead of trying to break into the industry as a poorly paid junior, Ella had gone for better-paid jobs. But this morning, sitting in a boutique Rome employment agency, Ella realised she could perhaps focus on herself.

'Sorry.' Claudia gave a helpless shrug and as Ella went to thank her, she halted her. 'One moment. We have a client, Corretti Media—they are in Sicily—Palermo. Have you heard of them?'

'A bit.' Ella was obsessed with the industry. 'They've done well with a few blockbusters recently.'

'Alessandro is the CEO, and there is Santo—he's a film producer.'

'I have heard of him.' Ella said, though chose not to add that it wasn't his producing skills he was famous for—more his scandalous ways. Still, Claudia seemed quite happy to discuss them.

'He goes through a lot of PAs!' Claudia rolled her eyes as she pulled up the file. 'Yes, it is Santo who is looking for someone—you would go with him when he is on location. You would need an open mind though—he is always getting into trouble and he has quite a reputation with women.'

Ella didn't care about his reputation, just the thought of being on location. Maybe she could get some experience—at least it would be a start. 'Perhaps he would be more forgiving of your Italian if I tell him that you are familiar with the industry.'

'My Italian is improving,' Ella said.

'And you'd need to seriously smarten up.'

This time Ella was offended. She was sitting in a very expensive grey suit—one that had been suitable for Parliament, she wanted to point out—but then again, it was three years old and politicians weren't exactly known for their stand-out fashion.

'Santo Corretti expects immaculate.'

Ella forced a smile. 'Then he'll get immaculate.'

'One moment.'

Ella sat as Claudia made the call, trying to quell the excitement that was mounting. Because for the first time she actually wanted a job, wanted it in a way she never had before, though her cheeks did burn a bit when Claudia looked her over and said that yes, she was good-looking. Was honey blonde hair really a prerequisite for this job? Ella wondered as she heard her hair being described.

As it turned out it didn't matter.

'Sorry...' Claudia shook her head. 'That was his current PA, and though she is very keen to leave, she says there is no point even putting you forward. He is very particular.'

'Well, thank you for trying.'

Leaving the agency Ella stopped for coffee. Gazing out the window at a busy Rome morning, she told herself it was ridiculous to be so disappointed about a job she hadn't even been interviewed for.

And even if she had... Ella looked out at the women. There was just an effortless elegance to them and if Santo Corretti went for immaculate then the bar was raised very high here in Italy. He would have taken one look at Ella in her rather boring interview suit and the answer would have been the same.

Anyway, Ella asked herself, did she really want to work in Sicily, did she really want to go and revisit her mother's past?

Yes.

Ella's heart started a frantic thump, because she simply wasn't ready. Except she was walking out of the café and instead of tackling the next agency on her list, she found herself peering into the beautifully dressed windows, wondering what a PA for Santo Corretti might wear. And a few moments later she was asking a shop assistant the same.

Well, she didn't say his name, just said that she had a very important job interview. A little while later Ella sat and had her long curly hair trimmed and tamed and then loosely tied at the nape and her make-up and nails done too.

By early afternoon she checked out of her hotel, and took the short flight to Sicily. She looked out at the land she had seen in endless faded photos that had been described to her over and over by her mother. Despite the beauty of the snowcapped mountains, the glistening azure sea and the juts of buildings vying for space on the coastline, Ella wasn't quite sure that she was ready for this. But she was here to work, she reminded herself.

While the bravest thing she had ever done might have been to leave Australia, Ella thought as she checked her luggage into storage and stepped out into the winter sun, this felt pretty brave too.

Or foolish.

She'd find out soon enough.

Ella climbed into a white taxi. 'Corretti Media.'

Ella held her breath, worried he might ask for an address, or say he had no idea where she meant, but the driver just nodded and Ella pulled out her mirror from her handbag, smoothed down her hair and touched up her make-up. Her newly capped gleaming white smile felt unfamiliar. No one would ever guess the price she had paid to get it—and not in money.

Snapping the mirror closed, Ella refused to dwell on it, just pushed all thoughts of her father aside. As the taxi pulled up outside the Corretti Media tower it was a very determined woman who paid the driver and then stepped into the sleek air-conditioned building and told the receptionist that she was here about the PA vacancy.

'Un attimo, prego.' The receptionist reached for her phone and a few moments later Ella stepped out of an elevator and was somewhat stunned by the response she received.

'Buona fortuna!' An exceptionally pretty and very tearful woman thrust a black leather-bound diary and a set of car keys at Ella as she wished her good luck dealing with Santo and then shouted over her shoulder an old Italian proverb that Ella had heard a few times from her mother. 'If a man deceives me once, shame on him. If he deceives me twice, shame on me.'

'I take it that's a no, then?'

A deep, rich voice had Ella turn and, as he walked out of his office, she could, for a dizzying second, understand his PA's willingness to have given this man a second chance. She clearly wasn't giving him a third for, with a sob, she ran for the door, leaving Ella alone with him.

Green eyes met hers and there was a hint of an unrepentant smile on a very beautiful mouth and, on his left cheek, a livid red hand print.

'Are you here for an interview?' he asked Ella in Italian and when she nodded and introduced herself, he gestured to his office and she followed him in.

He needed no introduction.

CHAPTER ONE

SANTO JERKED AWAKE, his heart racing, and reached out for familiar comfort, but rather than in bed with a lover beside him, he was asleep alone on a couch.

What happened last night?

His mind was a cruel trickster.

It did not tell him what had happened—it showed him little clues.

There was an empty whisky bottle on the floor, which Santo stepped over to get to the bathroom, and when he looked down he saw that he was still wearing the wedding suit, but his tie was off and the shirt torn and undone.

He checked the inside pocket of his jacket, remembered Ella double- and triple-checking that he had them before she left and he went off to be best man at his brother's wedding.

The rings were still there.

He splashed his face with water; his face and chest were a mass of bruises.

Santo looked at his neck and grimaced, but a few love bites were the least of his concerns as yesterday's events started to come back to him.

Alessandro!

Santo picked up the phone to arrange a driver, but he got the night receptionist who, perhaps unaware that she should not ask such questions, enquired where he wanted to go and Santo promptly hung up.

Looking out of the window, from his luxurious vantage point, Santo could see the press waiting. Rarely for Santo, he couldn't stomach facing them, or his brother, alone.

'Can you pick me up?

Despite the hour, Ella answered the phone with her eyes closed. After four months working for Santo Corretti she was more than used to being called out of hours, though he sounded particularly terrible this morning. His deep, low voice, thick with Italian accent, was still beautiful, if a touch hoarse.

Yes, beautiful and terrible just about summed Santo up.

Peeling her eyes open, she looked at the figures on her bedside clock. 'It's 6:00 a.m.,' Ella said. 'On a Sunday.' Which should have been enough reason to end the call and go back to sleep. Yet, all night, Ella had been half expecting him to ring, so much so she had sat with her giant heated rollers in last night and had already laid her clothes out. Like the rest of Sicily, Ella had watched the drama unfold on television yesterday afternoon and had seen updates on the news all night. Even her mother in Australia, watching the Italian news, would know that the much-anticipated wedding of Santo's brother, Alessandro Corretti, to Alessia Battaglia had been called off at the last minute.

Literally, at the last minute.

The bride had fled midway down the aisle and the

world was waiting to see how two of Sicily's most no-
torious families would deal with the fallout.

Yes, Ella had had a feeling that her services might
be required before Monday.

'Look, this is my day off.' She did her best to hold
firm. 'I worked yesterday...' Of course, as just his PA,
Ella hadn't been invited to the wedding. Instead her job
had been to ensure that Santo arrived sober, on time
and looking divine as he always did.

The divine part had been easy—Santo made a beautiful best man. It was the other two requisites that had
taken up rather a lot more of her people skills.

'I need to pick up Alessandro from the police station,' Santo said. 'He was arrested last night.'

Ella lay there silently, refusing to ask for details,
while privately wondering just what else had happened
yesterday.

She had raised a glass to the screen as she had seen
Santo arrive at the church, talking and joking with Alessandro, privately thinking that the gene pool had surely
been fizzing with expensive champagne when these
two were conceived.

They could, at first glance, almost be twins—both
were tall and broad shouldered, both wore their jet-black
hair short, both had come-to-bed dark green eyes—but
there were differences. Alessandro was the eldest, and
the two years that divided the brothers were significant.

As firstborn son to the late Carlo Corretti, Alessandro was rather more ruthless, whereas Santo was
a touch lighter in personality, more fun and extremely
flirty—but he could still be completely arrogant at
times.

'Come and pick me up now,' Santo said, as if to prove her point. Ella let out a long breath, telling herself that in a few weeks, if she got the job she had applied for, then all the scandal and drama of the Correttis would be a thing of the past. Working for Santo was nothing like she'd imagined it would be. 'The press are everywhere,' he warned, which was Santo's shorthand to remind her to look smart—even in a crisis he insisted on appearances. 'Take a taxi and then pick up my car and drive it around to the hotel entrance. Text me when you're there.'

'I hate driving your car,' Ella started, but was met again with silence. Having given his orders, Santo would assume she was jumping to the snap of his manicured fingers, and had already hung up.

'Bastard,' Ella hissed and then she heard his voice.

'You love me, really.'

Ella was too annoyed to be embarrassed. 'I love lying in on a Sunday morning.'

'Tough.'

This time he did hang up.

In a few weeks you'll be out of it, Ella told herself as she rang for a taxi. The woman on the other end of the phone sounded half asleep as well and told Ella it would be a good fifteen minutes to half an hour, which suited her fine. She climbed out of bed and headed straight for the shower and then to the mirror, but Santo could forget it if he thought she was going to arrive in full make-up. She changed her mind, because like it or not, Santo was her boss and Ella took her work very seriously. So, instead of a slick of mascara and lipgloss—which were usual weekend fare, if she wore any make-up at all—

Ella set to work with the make-up brushes and then smoothed out her hair a touch and tied it into a low ponytail. She pulled on a dark grey skirt and sheer cream blouse and added low heels.

One good thing about working for Santo was her clothing allowance.

Actually, it was the only good thing.

And Ella wasn't even particularly interested in clothes!

Hearing the taxi toot outside her small rented flat, Ella checked her appearance one more time and then grabbed her 'Santo Bag' as she called it, making sure that she had his spare set of car keys, before heading outside. She squinted at the morning sun and took in the vivid colours of a gorgeous Palermo in May. The ocean was glistening and the city still seemed to be sleeping. No doubt the whole of Sicily had had a late night, waiting for updates in the news.

'Buongiorno.' Ella gave the taxi driver the address of the smart hotel where Santo was staying and then sat back and listened to the morning news on the radio.

Of course the jilted Corretti groom was being talked about long after the headlines had been read.

And, of course, the taxi driver was more than delighted with the news. 'Trouble!' he told her. 'As if a wedding would ever unite the Corretti and Battaglia families...' and happily he chatted some more, unaware he was driving her to meet with Santo. Ella chose not to enlighten him. Santo didn't exactly keep her informed about the goings-on in his family. If anything, his Italian picked up pace if he ever had to speak with one of them, just enough to make it almost impossible for her to work out what was being said.

'They have always fought?' Ella checked.

'Always,' the driver told her and then added that even the death of Salvatore Corretti a few weeks ago would not bring peace between the two families. 'The Correttis even war with themselves.'

That much Ella knew. Even though Santo didn't reveal much about his family, Ella was forever having to deal with the feuding Corretti cousins. The family was incredibly divided and they were all constantly trying to outdo the other, under the guise of the family empire. They were all trying to outmanoeuvre one another in the bid to become top dog, not just at work, but with cars, with women, with horses. Ella was sick of it. She was tired of the dark secrets and mind games they all played.

She'd have put up with it for a while longer though, if Santo would just give her a small step onto the ladder she wanted to climb. Over and over she had asked him if she could work on just one of his films as a junior assistant director.

'Presto,' Santo would say and then, as he did all too often when he spoke to her in Italian, he would annoyingly translate for her. 'Soon.'

Well, soon, she'd be gone.

Ella asked the driver to stop while she bought some coffee and then climbed back in.

As they approached the hotel Ella told the driver that she wished to be dropped off in the underground car park. As they approached she saw that Santo was right—there were a lot of press around and security was tight. Ella was more than happy to show her ID before paying the taxi driver and telling the concerned valet that she wanted to personally take the car up to collect her boss.

Ella slipped into the front seat and smelt not the leather, but the familiar, expensive scent of Santo. Before she started the engine she texted him, letting him know she was in the basement and on her way to collect him.

The engine growled at the merest touch of her foot and she jerked her way through the car park, doing her best to ignore the flash of cameras as the paparazzi stirred at the new activity taking place.

Come on, Santo, she muttered as she sat with the engine idling, glad of the effort she'd made as cameras clicked away, worried, too, that he might have fallen back to sleep after he had called her. But then, still wearing last night's suit, she saw him, walking just a little unsteadily towards the car. Ella's lips pressed together when she saw the state he was in. The press were going to have a field day. His suit was torn and dirty and he was wearing several fresh bruises too. His deathly pale skin only accentuated the fact that he hadn't shaved.

'*Buongiorno!*' Ella said loudly and brightly as he climbed in.

'Good morning, Ella.'

It was a small game that they played, one that they had partaken in since her interview. Ella, determined to show him how wonderful her Italian was, attempting to prove that just because she was Australian it didn't mean that she wasn't up for the job, had introduced herself in her very best Italian.

Santo had promptly responded in English—pulling rank and basically saying that his English was better than her Italian, which was of course right. Though, as it turned out, Ella did speak enough Italian to land the job. But when it was just the two of them, they conversed mainly in English, except for this one mutual game.

'I thought you wanted us looking smart.'

He just frowned.

'You said there were press everywhere.'

'There are,' Santo said. 'I was just warning you.'

'Here.' She handed him his coffee.

'You need to get one for Alessandro,' Santo said.

'I already did.'

'Let's go then.'

They jerked out of the forecourt. 'Why do you have to have gears?' Ella moaned, because she always drove an automatic, though of course Santo didn't consider that real driving. Still, he didn't answer, just sat, unusually quiet, as the car moved out into the bright sunlight. Glancing over she watched him wince and, taking mild pity, Ella put her hand in her Santo Bag and handed him a pair of sunglasses. But even they didn't fully cover the purple bruise on his eye.

As the press surged, Ella inched gingerly forward, aware that one slip of her foot on Santo's accelerator could flatten the lot of them.

'Just go!' Santo cursed as they gathered for their shots and then he cursed again as Ella blasted the horn a few times and finally dispersed them.

His mood didn't improve as they drove through

town. 'I hate driving in this country,' Ella muttered as she was forced to swerve and narrowly missed a Vespa. In Australia they drove on the left-hand side of the road and occasionally they even managed to follow the road rules.

Though it wasn't the traffic that was getting to Ella, nor the 6:00 a.m. wake-up call from her boss, whatever fight he had been in last night didn't account for the purple marks on his neck.

Bloody hell, she thought darkly, even in the middle of a family scandal, even as the Battaglia and Corretti families exploded, trust Santo to still be at it.

With who though?

No, Ella was not going to ask for details.

She really didn't want to know if he'd run true to form and gotten off with Taylor Carmichael, the stunning American actress who was playing the leading role in the latest film Santo was producing.

Shooting started on Monday and Santo had made it his personal mission to keep Taylor out of trouble. He had insisted that she attend yesterday's wedding to both ensure that Taylor behaved and to garner some publicity for the film. But with both their reputations, it was perhaps a forgone conclusion as to what had taken place.

It really was time to move on. If she didn't get the new job, then maybe she could head to London, or France perhaps.

Or even go home?

He asked her to stop so that he could draw out some cash to hopefully expedite getting his brother out of the lock-up and Ella closed her eyes and leant her head back on the headrest. The thought of home brought no comfort at all. It was her mother's birthday in a few days and Ella would be expected to call. She was gripped with sudden panic at the thought and opened her eyes and took a couple of deep breaths as she realised that no, she was nowhere near ready to go home.

She watched as Santo had a few attempts at the machine and then, with an irritated sigh, Ella climbed out of the car and walked over to him, tapping his number in.

'What would I do without you?' There was no endearment in his question. He turned his head for a moment and Ella felt heat rise on her cheeks, but then told herself that there was no challenge behind his words. There was no way Santo could know what she had been up to in recent days.

And, Ella consoled herself, who in her position wouldn't be looking for another job? She was tired of bailing him out, tired because now she'd had to get up at some ridiculous hour on her one day off to bail his brother out. Tired, too, of running Santo's not-so-little black book—sending flowers and jewellery to his girl-friends, booking intimate tables in fantastic restaurants, organising romantic weekends and then having to calm ruffled feathers when invariably, inevitably, Santo upset them in his oh-so-usual way.

'How was Taylor?' She simply couldn't stop herself from asking, because it was imperative for the film publicity that Taylor had behaved herself last night.

'Niente dichiarazione,' Santo responded, smiling at her pursed lips. 'I am practising "no comment" for the press today. Perhaps you could practise too.'

He was so good at deflecting questions, not just

about women, about everything. Always managing to shrug off things that should matter but simply didn't to Santo.

As they pulled up at the police station, Ella was relieved that there were no press waiting; at least word hadn't got out yet that Alessandro was here.

'How do you think he'll be?'

'Hungover.' Santo yawned. 'And far better off without her.'

He went to climb out and Ella, who'd assumed that she'd be sitting for half an hour, or however long it took to bail someone out, was surprised when Santo turned around and asked if she would come in with him.

'Me?' Ella checked.

'You might sweeten up the *polizia*.'

'I find that really offensive, Santo.'

'Ah, but you find so many things really offensive, Ella,' he drawled.

Ella collected Allesandro's coffee and walked towards the police station with Santo. She knew exactly what that little dig had been about—Ella was the first PA he hadn't slept with. She had made it clear, to his obvious surprise, that this was business only. To his credit he had backed off completely, but now and then there was a little dig, a tiny reference to the fact she was resistant to his charms.

Not completely, of course.

No woman could be. He was stunning to look at and incredibly sexy, but completely incorrigible. Yes, a night with the boss might be tempting at times, especially when he smiled, especially when he looked as impossibly beautiful as he did today. But it was the thought of the morning after that, for Ella, was enough to ensure she resisted.

They stepped into the station and there was a lot of talking, a lot of hand waving and the handing over of an awful lot of cash, but, surprisingly quickly, a very dishevelled Alessandro appeared. He had his share of bruises too and there were grazes over his knuckles and that oh-so-immaculate bridegroom suit was covered in dust and torn.

'Here.' Ella handed him his coffee, which was no doubt cold by now, but Alessandro drained it in one go as they walked back out of the police station. He winced at the far-too-bright morning sunlight that seemed to be magnified by the ocean, and Ella handed him a pair of sunglasses too—she always carried spares.

Ella wasn't Santo's PA for nothing!

'Thank you,' Alessandro said. Putting them on he looked at his brother, taking in the bruises and thick lip and the nasty graze on Santo's cheek. 'What happened to your face?'

Ella held her breath.

She was dying to know, but the answer served only to surprise and further confuse her.

'You did,' came Santo's wry response.

CHAPTER TWO

'You don't remember?' Santo asked, once they were in the car and Alessandro had asked Ella to drive him to his home.

'I am trying not to.'

They were speaking in Italian, but Ella could pretty much make out all that was being said.

'I spent the whole night trying to contact you,' Santo said.

'Clearly, not the whole night,' came Alessandro's terse response. 'Who the hell did you let loose on your neck?'

Santo just laughed and offered no explanation. 'I must have rung you fifty times.'

'And forty-nine times I chose not to answer.' Alessandro withdrew into silence and Ella didn't blame him. Santo, it would seem, had not a care in the world. He just scrolled through the endless ream of texts on his phone as they talked, ignoring the constant buzzes to alert him to a call.

Ella drove them to the Corretti Media tower, where Alessandro had a luxurious penthouse, but the paparazzi were still clamouring for their shot of the jilted groom.

'Lie down in the back if you want,' Ella suggested.

'I brought a coat for you. I'll try to get in the back way.' But Alessandro refused her suggestion to lie down, told her to just drop him at the front and sat there stony faced as the cameras flashed and reporters shouted their questions.

'I'll come in with you,' Santo said.

'I don't need a handhold,' came Alessandro's terse response, but Santo ignored him and when she stopped the car both the brothers got out.

The gathered press went into a frenzy. Both were, Ella knew, more than used to dealing with them. There were always questions and scandal where this family was concerned. But though there were questions that would certainly need to be answered, interviews that would have to be given and the press to be faced, clearly, for Alessandro, it was all just a little too soon. Ella watched as a rather personal question was asked and Alessandro's shoulders stiffened, his hands balling into two fists. Perhaps Santo realised that his brother was very close to losing his temper again, because for once, Santo made a very sensible choice and turned his brother back towards the vehicle. Ella reached out and opened the door and Santo shoved his fuming brother into the back of the car before climbing into the front.

'Drive on,' Santo said. 'Get around the corner, and then I will drive.' He was clearly impatient by Ella's rather tentative speed and once around the corner Santo reminded her that he had asked her to pull over.

'Fine, but if you're driving I'm getting out. I can smell the whisky from here.'

For once he didn't offer a smart retort, just gestured

for her to carry on, and turning the car around at the first opportunity, she drove the trio back into town.

'We can go to the hotel you are staying at,' Ella suggested to Santo. 'We can enter via the basement.'

'No,' Alessandro said. 'I'm not going to be holed up somewhere by the press. I just want away from them.'

'We could go to mine.' Ella tried to think how best to give Alessandro privacy for a few days, though she could hardly imagine him staying at her cheap rental place. 'It's just a small villa, but it's pretty tucked away, so I'm sure that they'd never think to look for you there.'

Ella glanced in the mirror as she awaited his response, but instead of answering her, Alessandro spoke briefly to his brother, who argued with him for a moment.

But then Santo spoke. 'Take him to the harbour at Cala Marina.' Santo gave her directions. 'Alessandro wants to go to his yacht.'

Ella did as she was told, heading to the harbour where Alessandro's yacht was docked. But despite her resolve to refuse to ask for details and despite reminding herself that it was none of her business as the car ate up the miles, on this, Ella couldn't stay silent. 'Do you really think that's such a good idea?' She turned worried eyes to Santo. Ella really didn't like the idea of Alessandro alone on a yacht, given all that had happened.

'I have just been reminded that I am the younger brother.' Santo scratched at his neck and then pulled at his unbuttoned collar as if it was a little too tight. 'He insists that we take him or he shall arrange his own transport there.'

Which gave them no choice—they were hardly going

to let Alessandro out on the street to make his own way. So they drove, pretty much in silence, till they neared the pretty harbour. Ella almost willed one of the brothers to start talking so she could find out just a little of what had taken place last night, but perhaps because she was there, neither spoke about family matters.

'*Dove Alessia?*' For the first time Alessandro initiated conversation, asking where his ex-fiancée was, and Ella held her breath as they pulled into the harbour.

'*Puttana,*' came Santo's crude and dismissive response, but Alessandro was insistent.

'Where is she?'

And Ella was still holding her breath when Santo answered his brother, telling him the truth in a very dismissive voice—that it would seem that Alessia and their cousin Matteo had run off together.

The expletive that came from Alessandro was perhaps merited, and unlike Santo, he was nice enough to give a brief apology to Ella for his language before leaving the car and staggering off towards his yacht.

Santo sat for a moment and watched his brother and then climbed out of the car, trying, Ella presumed, to persuade Alessandro to come back with them.

She watched them argue for a moment but the bond between the two brothers was clear. It mattered not that Alessandro had thrown a few punches at Santo last night. It didn't change anything between them. Not for the first time Ella wondered what it would be like to have a sibling, how it might feel to have someone in your corner—for how it hurt to deal with her parents alone.

But whatever Santo said to his brother, it didn't work.

Alessandro shrugged him off and she watched as Santo stood for a moment, then turned around. But instead of a roll of the eyes and the slightly cocky smile Santo often wore, his face was grey as he walked back towards the car and climbed in.

They sat for a moment and watched Alessandro board his yacht.

'Do you think he'll be all right?' Ella was loath to leave.

'Of course,' Santo said. 'He's tough.'

He'd need to be tough—being jilted at the altar with the world's cameras aimed on him, Ella thought. 'Santo, I don't know that it's right to leave him.'

'Just drive.' Again Santo dismissed her worries. 'He'll be fine.'

She couldn't believe his lack of concern, but that was Santo. He dealt with stuff as it cropped up and then moved easily on to the next thing, never worrying about the chaos he was leaving behind.

Ella rang ahead and asked housekeeping to sort out his suite and run a bath and asked for some breakfast and a lot of coffee to be sent up.

'Assuming that your company won't mind,' Ella checked, telling herself that she wasn't fishing for answers.

'She's gone.'

'Just the one?' Ella glanced over, thinking she'd get a glimpse of a smile, but Santo was just staring out of his window.

The press were still waiting but Santo didn't duck. He just sat there as they got their shots. As Ella went to indicate, to enter the hotel via the more secure route of the basement, Santo stopped her.

'The foyer will be fine—I don't need the basement.' In fact, he took off his dark glasses and pocketed them before he got out, hurling a filthy look straight in the direction of the cameras before stalking into the hotel with his head held high. Ella threw the car keys to the valet and caught up with him at the lift. As the doors closed behind them, Santo slumped against the wall for a moment, his eyes closed, and Ella was no longer just worried about Alessandro—no, she was more than a little concerned for Santo too. He was incredibly pale. Assuming that it was Alessandro who had hit him last night, then it was one very angry fist Santo would have found himself at the end of—maybe he'd been knocked out?

'Are you hurt anywhere else?'

He didn't open his eyes, just shook his head.

'Were you knocked out?' Ella checked.

'Unfortunately, no.' Green eyes opened and he gave a thin smile and she found herself staring back to a different Santo. It was as if all the arrogance had left him, as if, for once, she was seeing the man he really was and it was mesmerising. She simply could not stop staring—even as the lift doors opened—and for a moment the two of them just stood.

'What happened?' She had sworn not to ask, yet she did.

'Why?'

'I just…' She flailed for words. 'I'm concerned.'

'Sure you are!' There was an edge to his words that told her he considered her a liar. For a moment she was confused, but now wasn't the time to dwell on it. Instead they walked to his suite. Of course, he couldn't find his swipe card but, of course, she carried a spare.

As they stepped into the suite it was scandal rather than breakfast that awaited. Santo thumbed through the papers and Ella gave in and picked up one. Perhaps, she consoled herself, it was better that Alessandro was on a boat and escaping all this, for the photos and write-ups were brutal.

'Oh!' Ella let out a small crow of shock at one particular photo. There was Taylor Carmichael, the woman Santo should have been policing yesterday, the actress who he was relying on to behave, running true to form despite promises that she had changed.

'Is it any surprise?' Santo shrugged.

Probably not, Ella conceded. In fact, her only surprise was that the man in the image wasn't Santo. But did he care about nothing? Filming started tomorrow and there had been a lot of fireworks about the casting of the leading female role. Taylor's comeback after a spectacular unravelling was risky at best—a disaster for the film at worst.

And this looked like it was turning into a complete disaster.

Still, problems with the film would have to wait till tomorrow. Right now Ella had more pressing things to sort out—like six-foot-three of beaten-up, hungover male. 'Go and have a bath,' Ella said. 'I'll chase breakfast.'

'I don't want breakfast' was his inevitable response. 'I'm just going to go to bed. Thanks for all your help.'

'You have to eat something,' Ella started, and then

shut up. After all, she wasn't his mother. Not that his own mother would be worrying too much—Carmela Corretti's only concerns were fashion and manicures.

'Just have a bath.' Ella settled for, 'I don't care whether or not you eat. I for one happen to be starving, so I'm chasing them.'

'Sure.'

He headed to the bathroom and after a few minutes there was a knock at the door and Ella stood as the maid set up the table.

'Thank you,' Ella said, pouring herself a coffee and trying not to overthink who he'd been with last night. It was none of her business what Santo got up to.

She flicked through the papers, reading some of the more salacious details that had come out. They were the most complicated of families and for a while she was lost in the gossip. But later, glancing at the bedside clock, Ella realised he'd been in there ages. She thought maybe he had fallen asleep and she tried to ignore the knot of worry in her stomach, but after a moment or two she knocked.

'Breakfast is here.'

Ella stood at the door and all she could hear was silence.

'Santo…' She knocked again. 'Answer me.'

Nothing.

'Santo!' Ella tried to keep the note of panic from her voice as she thought of head injuries and hangovers and the fact that the newspaper headlines could be far worse tomorrow than they were now. She was actually terrified for him.

'Santo!' She rapped loudly. 'If you don't answer then I'm going to have to come in.'

Still nothing.

Ella tried the handle, but of course it was locked.

Heart in her mouth she ran to her bag, rummaging through it and then through her purse to find a coin. With shaking fingers, she fitted it into the slot and turned the lock.

'Santo!' she shouted and when still there was no response, Ella knew she had no choice but to go in.

CHAPTER THREE

'Santo…' As soon as she opened the door, Ella regretted it.

There were some things she simply shouldn't see and immediately Ella knew why he hadn't answered her.

Santo's modesty was covered by bubbles, his head resting on the edge of the bath. His eyes were screwed closed, and his lips were pressed together. For once Ella wasn't catching her boss doing something inappropriate—that she could deal with. What she couldn't immediately deal with was the fact that Santo Corretti, a man who charmed his way through life, who always had a smart answer for everything, who, she was sure, cared about nothing other than movies and getting laid, was lying in a bath and trying and failing not to cry.

Santo never cried.

He could not remember a single time that he had. It was an entirely new experience to him.

Not when his father, Carlo, had died alongside his uncle. Nor had there been a hint of a tear at his grandfather's death. Not even as a little boy—it was as if he'd been born knowing that tears would never work with his mother, Carmela, and any sign of weakness would only have infuriated Carlo. So instead Santo had relied solely on looks, wit and charm.

He'd just run out them today.

'Go...' He put his hand up, the word barely making it out of his lips, his shoulders shaking with the effort of holding it in. Both wished they were embarrassed for a rather more salacious reason.

'I can't just go.' And no, this wasn't in her job description, but Ella wasn't just going to leave him, so she sat on the edge of the bath and pondered the man. He was unshaven, there were bruises on his chest too and he looked battered but not just physically—he looked broken.

She had at times wondered if there were any feelings to be had in that beautiful head, but now he lay clearly shattered and she watched as he blew out a breath and then finally spoke.

'Do you really think he'll be okay?'

'It's Alessandro!' Ella said firmly. 'Which means yes—of course he'll be fine. He just needs some time.'

After a moment Santo nodded and then opened his eyes. Ella didn't want him to be so beautiful, but seeing this side of him just served to confuse her more. 'I really do think that he'll be fine.'

'It's not just Alessandro...' he admitted. 'It's the whole lot of them. You should have heard the stuff that came out last night,' Santo started, but didn't continue.

'You can tell me.'

'Because you care?' There was a strange surliness to his words and Ella frowned, but then he shrugged. 'It is family stuff—it is not for me to say.'

Ella chose not to push. She knew all about family

secrets, knew there were certain things you just didn't speak about. She had lived her life keeping quiet after all.

She looked around the bathroom and wondered how someone could make so much mess in so little time. His clothes were strewn all over the floor, the tap was still running where Santo had brushed his teeth and no, she noted he didn't replace the cap.

'It's a mess,' Santo said, only she guessed that he wasn't talking about the bathroom.

'Families often are.'

She looked at him then, met his eyes. Usually she pulled hers away, usually she could not stand to have anyone examine her soul. But she saw the green and the bloodshot and the pain in his and for a second she thought she might cry too, which she hadn't since that terrible day. As Ella sat looking at Santo she was a breath away from telling him that she knew the pain the people who should love you the most could cause, but she held on to it, just as she always had.

He did not ask.

She did not tell.

It was safer that way.

'Come on,' Ella finally said. She knew that he would hate to have been seen like this, knew that neither would mention it again.

She put her hand in the water and met his ankle, but she brushed past that and pulled out the plug. Then standing she turned off the sink tap. But as she went to go, Santo just lay there, the water rather rapidly disappearing, and before she saw far too much of her boss Ella grabbed a towel.

'I'll avert my gaze,' Ella said, holding the towel up while trying to make a joke, but there was simply no room for jokes this morning and no room for modesty either. In the end, Santo took her hand and sort of hauled himself out of the bath as Ella did her best not to look. He tucked the towel around his hips and walked out to the suite, bypassing the breakfast that had been laid out and heading straight to bed.

'Sorry about this.'

'Oh, you will be…' Ella started and then stopped. Now really wasn't a time for their regular teasing. 'Let's just forget about it.' He gave her a slightly suspicious look, but Ella meant it. Yes, they might tease each other at times, but she wasn't going to use this. 'It never happened, Santo.'

'Thanks.' He gave a brief nod and then went back to telling her what to do. 'Can you get my phone?'

He sat on the edge of the bed as Ella went off and he could hear her loading up plates and pouring drinks. Santo really did not know what was happening to him— it was as if everything had suddenly caught up, everything he had pushed down and ignored or suppressed was now strewn out before him and refused to go back into its neat box. Family secrets spewing out last night had made Santo feel physically sick. For the first time he hadn't even been able to screw his way out of it— last night he had removed his mouth from hers, felt her lips on his neck and looked down at another nameless blonde and couldn't be fagged to head to bed. Instead he had sent her on her way and spent the night with a bottle of whisky, trying to get hold of Alessandro.

Santo sat there searching for one good area of his life,

but even the film was in trouble now thanks to Taylor's behaviour yesterday.

One good thing.

He looked up as Ella walked in, his very professional, somewhat aloof PA, and very annoyed suddenly, Santo climbed into bed and tossed the towel to the floor in a very surly gesture because, apart from the drama of his family, he'd found another thing out yesterday.

'You're leaving?'

Ella felt a blush spread over her cheeks, and it wasn't because he was clearly naked beneath the sheets. There was the awful part when looking for another job where you naturally didn't let your employer know. She had felt such horrible guilt as she'd lied about her where-abouts and, to make matters worse, Santo had been re-ally nice about her trip to Rome to supposedly visit a doctor. He'd paid for her flight and even put her up in a luxurious hotel overnight. Ella understood now a couple of the barbs that had come her way this morning. She'd offered him the chance to speak about his family when he'd known that she was already planning to leave.

Ella walked over and actually sat on the edge of the bed and looked at his scowling face. 'I don't know for sure if I'm leaving yet,' she said.

'That trip to Rome wasn't for the doctors...' She blushed darker as he said it. 'The film industry is a tight one, Ella—people talk.'

'I don't even know if I've got the job.'

'Well, it sounds like you have. Luigi rang yesterday for your references,' Santo said. 'You'll forgive me if I don't offer my congratulations.'

And she wanted more details but, given the situation,

it would be unfair to ask for them. She daren't get her hopes up either, not till Luigi contacted her. Maybe all it would be was an invite for a second interview. 'Can we talk about this later?'

'We'll talk about it now.' Santo glared at her. 'I understand you want to be a director—I get that you want some involvement—but the director I have hired for this movie comes with his own team.' He took a breath, realised that he did not want to lose her. 'When I hire for the next movie, I will make it a priority to see if whomever I hire—'

'I wanted in on this movie, Santo.' Ella looked at him. 'I love the script so much, you know that.'

'And you know how important this film is to me, Ella, even more so now.'

'Now?'

'I am not going into that, other than to say I am not taking any risks with it.'

'Unless it's a risk called Taylor Carmichael,' Ella snapped.

'And look how that risk has paid off? But I will consider you for the next one.'

'It's not just that.' Ella closed her eyes. When you were Santo's PA there was plenty of other stuff to complain about. 'I don't get a moment....' She looked at him. 'You're way more than a full-time job, Santo.'

'This was an exception. I do not ring you usually on a Sunday.'

'Santo, Sunday starts at midnight on a Saturday night, so actually, quite often, you do.'

This was her job, Santo consoled himself as he sat there, but he knew he had been pushing things this weekend. Though he would never admit it out loud, he did concede that he had been nervous about the wedding, at the two families in the same church and the reception afterwards. Spending yesterday morning with Ella had been somewhat soothing.

Today, facing his brother, he had wanted her alongside.

'You've become indispensable.'

'No,' Ella said, refusing to give in to him. Santo had a way with words and was very good at saying the right thing when he wanted his own way. 'No one is.'

'Perhaps,' Santo said, and then thought for a moment. 'We get on.'

'Not all of the time.'

'I thought we did—we have had some laughs.'

She looked at his depraved face, at a man who so easily made her laugh and had no idea what a feat that was—no idea how tender and bruised her soul had been when she had first met him. That the smile she had worn for her interview had been false on so many levels. Of course she could share that with no one and so Ella looked down, took a croissant from the plate and peeled a piece off and then popped it in her mouth, aware that he was closely watching.

'I thought you were about to feed me.'

She was glad to see the slight return to his humour.

'Not a chance.' She gave him a weak smile as he checked his phone. 'Any messages?'

'Nothing.'

She could see the worry in the set of his lips. 'I didn't realise you and Alessandro were so close.'

'We're brothers,' Santo said, as if that explained everything. 'Do you have a brother or sister?'

'Nope—just me.' He noticed the slight strain to her voice, and he should have left it, really, except he did not.

'You hardly ever speak of your family.'

'Because we hardly ever speak.'

'How come?' Santo asked, but Ella shook her head. She just wasn't going to go there with him. It was time she left the room now and so once he'd eaten a croissant and drained his coffee she took the tray and stood.

'Is there anything else I can do for you?'

'You know there is.'

Yes, his humour was back!

'Get some sleep,' Ella said and turned off the hotel phone by his bedside. Then she headed over and drew the drapes, more than a little aware that Santo was watching her. She was just too aware of him too much of the time. As she glanced down she could see the press outside the hotel, still hovering, and she knew that this wasn't going to go away any time soon.

'Okay.' She walked back over to the bed. 'I'll leave you till about two.'

'You're staying?'

'I'll do some work in the lounge.'

'Come in and check my pulse.'

'No, but I will answer your phone. Is there any comment you want me to give?'

'I'll deal with all of that.'

As she went to take his phone from the bedside he stopped her, his hand closing over hers. 'No.'

'I'll deal with the calls,' Ella said. 'Santo, that's what

you pay me for. If it's Alessandro I'll bring the phone straight through to you.' She was terribly aware of his hand over hers, and more so when still it remained. She should simply have lifted her hand and walked out the room, as she would have on any other day, except she didn't and neither did she resist when he pulled her back to sit on the bed. With the curtains drawn it was unlike before—dark and more intimate and too much for her racing heart.

'Do you have to leave?'

'Santo, please...' Ella really didn't want to talk about it now. 'I have to think about my career. Can we...?'

'I meant, do you have to leave the room?'

'You didn't mean that.' Ella blushed as he smiled. Usually she rebuffed any flirting easily. It was just a little harder to do this morning and not just because they were on a bed in a very dark room, more because she felt as if she had glimpsed today the real Santo, the one behind the very expensive but very shallow facade.

'I would miss you.'

'For a little while.' Ella smiled.

'There could be advantages though....' As he spoke, Ella's heart thumped in her chest, knew what he was leading up to. 'Remember how you told me you would never get involved with someone you work with?'

'I do.'

Her second day at work, they had gone for dinner after, had sat side by side and pored through his diary, Ella taking notes, trying to be efficient but terribly aware of his beauty and trying to ignore it, just trying to work, when his hand had reached for her face.

She'd tried to emulate the hairdresser, had done everything they had said, except her curls hadn't been quite so glossy and kept escaping the hair tie. She'd felt his hand move to her cheek, his fingers capturing a lock of her hair.

'Don't.'

Refreshingly he hadn't made an excuse and neither had he apologised as he dropped contact. Instead he'd asked a question. 'Why?' His eyes had frowned a little, a curious smile on his lips at her response. No doubt it was one he wasn't used to.

'I don't have to give an answer to that.' Ella had more than met his eyes. 'But if you try anything like that again, you'll have my notice with immediate effect.'

How she rued those words now.

'We have a problem,' Santo said and she looked at him. Though it was terribly hard to think of Santo and morals at the same time, Ella realised, he did actually have some. For apart from a few stunning suggestions, apart from the odd gentle flirt, not once since that day had he put so much as a finger wrong.

She just wanted him to put that finger wrong now.

And he did.

Just one finger dusted her forearm and Santo waited for her hand to halt his, gave her every opportunity to stand, to change her mind. She'd been very clear as to her boundaries, but his breath stilled as he felt them tumble down.

Hell had been the night, and the morning pure misery, but now... He felt the tiny hairs on her arm rise beneath the pads of his fingers and the constant shiver between them deepen as her silence let him go on.

'Immediate effect...' Santo said and he wasn't checking her leaving date, more the flare of her skin to his, but she did appreciate the check-in. All she wanted now was to find out how it felt to be kissed by a man as expert and beautiful as Santo.

'I already told you—today never happened.'

He was wary to move too fast and kiss her, and anyway, there was more that his hand wanted to do. It moved up to her neck, his fingers to her cheek, and it lingered a long time on that same lock of hair, where once she had halted him, and then to lips that had never met his. He felt them, slowly explored them.

Ella sat there, her heart pounding, because she had never expected this. She had never known fingers on her lips could be so sensual. Oh, she had heard much about the man, had dreamt about him a little more than she would ever admit to, but she had just never thought of him like this.

She had never thought that he might be slow and unhurried and make her burn between her legs without even offering his mouth.

His fingers worked the flesh of her lips as if he were stroking her below, teasing and worrying the curve of her Cupid's bow. Then he slipped his finger in and she caught it loosely with her teeth and licked around it, sucked lightly on it. Her tease worked too, because Santo pulled her to him then and replaced his fingers with his tongue. It was a very deep, intimate kiss, his tongue lolling around hers. His hand was on her head, pushing her deeper towards him.

It was, Ella thought as she sank beneath his hand, as if they had kissed five hundred times before, for both knew exactly what the other wanted. She loved the noise of them, the moan he sighed into her mouth. But just as she went to end it, just when she knew she had to, his other hand found her breast and, not in the least bit tenderly, he stroked it. She succumbed to his palm and fingers for there was nothing subtle and as her body responded she was very aware that he was naked beneath the bedding and also, thanks to earlier, very aware as to how delicious the view was under there.

Just when she should leave, when she should stop this, just as her face went to move back, Santo read it. He chased her with his mouth, reached now for her hips and guided her to a stand, a stand where she was bending and kissing him. When she stopped, he did not let her retreat, because the magic of his mouth had her kneeling on the bed and the implicit message from his hands had her lying on top of him, looking down at him.

'Where were we?' He smiled. 'Oh, that's right...' and he got back to kissing. And even though it was Ella dressed and on top, she felt as if she were naked beneath, for he had completely taken her over, his hands sliding over her bottom, pressing her in. Then he moved her a fraction, till she was perfectly poised, and he lifted his hips as his hands shifted her.

It was supposed to be a kiss, but he was filthy and indecent and just so good. It really was supposed to have been just a kiss except his fingers had undone her skirt and his hands now slid in and cupped her bottom and still he moved her.

'Santo.' She tried to halt him, had no idea the fire she'd been playing with. She'd known he'd be good, but Ella just hadn't been prepared for how good he was. In just a few minutes her body felt scalded, and in no time at all she wanted to tear at her clothes just for the relief of being naked. She was grappling for control here and fast realising that with Santo she had none.

'Come on, Ella…' He was hurrying her for a reason. He wanted her to come so that two minutes later he could, because Santo knew the second he was inside he'd explode. His hand was working the curves that had taunted him for months now and he wanted to spend the day making up for lost time. Finally there was one good thing to hold on to and hold on to it he did, squeezing and digging his fingers into her buttocks, grinding his hips up to hers. He was just lost in the reprieve from the hell she had given him, so lost that it took a second to realise that she had stopped kissing him He looked up to Ella as she lifted her head, his hands stilling as the once-mutual rhythm stopped.

'Get some sleep.' She was as breathless as he.

'Don't do that to me.' Santo grinned and pressed into her again.

'I am doing that.'

'Ella!'

'It's a kiss, Santo…' she attempted, because it had been so very much more. 'It doesn't always have to lead to something.' Except her body said otherwise, but she was not going to lose her head to him. She reminded herself why—he was a rake, and an unrepentant rake at that. 'Have you seen the state of your neck?' she sweetly said. 'I find it a bit off-putting.'

'Nothing happened last night.'

He felt her disbelieving half-laugh, felt it reverberate through him as her breasts lay heavy and warm on his chest. 'Actually, it's true. I got so bored kissing her, midway my mind wandered.' It was terrible that he could make her laugh. 'Next thing I knew she was leeched onto my neck.'

'You should pay more attention.'

She was reminded of the placement of his hands as his fingers stroked her buttocks gently and then ventured just a little further to her centre. 'Oh, I'll pay attention, miss.'

So tempting was that thought she almost conceded, but no, it was supposed to have been just a kiss and Ella needed her head, needed to think, and with Santo lying naked beneath her, it wasn't a very doable ask.

'Go to sleep.' She gave him a light kiss on the lips but did not linger. She prised her body from his and stood, did up her skirt with hands that were shaking and made no effort to tuck her blouse in, just collected the phone. But as she reached the door his voice caught her.

'Could you pass me the tissues?'

'You know what, Santo?' Ella was at the door. 'You just take things too far sometimes.'

'Sorry?' She heard the question in his voice and then he laughed. 'I want to blow my nose. It's a curious thing this crying. I've never done it before. I feel like I have a cold.'

'Liar!' Ella said, and threw him the box.

He caught it and then his words caught her again at the door. 'But if you change your mind…'

CHAPTER FOUR

SHE WOULD NOT be changing her mind, so instead Ella headed out of the bedroom and, closing the door, poured herself a glass of grapefruit juice. She liked the tart taste on her tongue but it did not quench her, because her mouth still thrummed from his attention. The skin on her face was still alive from the drag of his jaw and there was a triangle of ache from her nipples that pointed down. The heavy bedroom door might just as well be made of paper, because it would be so easy to walk through it.

Ella was the most focused, determined person where her work was concerned, and certainly wouldn't let any man get in the way.

Not even one as drop-dead gorgeous as Santo.

Especially not one as drop-dead gorgeous as Santo.

Ella was well aware she attracted bastards—a couple of relationships had taught her that—only Santo wasn't actually one.

He never made promises he had no intention of keeping. His reputation served as enough of a warning and fool was the woman who might think he would change.

Ella wasn't a fool.

She's simply refused to give in to the want that sometimes curled inside when he was around. Her career came first, but this morning, knowing she was perhaps leaving, for a few dangerous moments she had given in.

And look at the consequences.

It was supposed to have been a kiss. She hadn't been prepared for the chemistry lab to ignite.

Ella spent the morning fielding calls, trying not to think of the man lying naked in bed just metres away, but in the end she gave in talking on the phone. She was sick of the name Taylor Carmichael, sick to her stomach about the questions being asked about Santo's family, and so she diverted all calls, except any from Alessandro. She turned on Santo's computer and, logging into the account she had on there, she checked her emails, her heart stopping for a moment when she saw that Luigi, the man who had interviewed her over a week ago, had finally replied.

She sped through the polite chatter at the beginning of the email, where he apologised for taking so long, and then she read the news she had been waiting for—in a month's time she would be junior assistant director on an upcoming film that was being shot in both Rome and Florence.

Everything seemed to stop for a moment. She had waited for this for so long—okay, it was a junior assistant director's role, which was probably more like a barista, but she had a title and she would be doing more than she was doing now. Santo was so fierce about his films, so protective of them, and she didn't really blame him for not giving her a chance.

Ella closed her eyes as her mind wandered back to the man in the bedroom.

She knew a lot about Santo's relationships—they were in days and weeks at best. A brief flash of devotion was all any woman got from Santo—a swamp of texts and phone calls, dinner, bed, breakfast, flowers, champagne. Ella paid his bills and did the bookings after all, and then, just as quickly as it all started, it would be over...and left to Ella to field phone calls and mop tears.

The hotel phone trilled. It was reception wondering what time Santo would be checking out or if he would be staying another night and Ella answered it, cold from a lack of sleep last night and stiff from sitting in the chair.

'I'm not sure.' When you were speaking on behalf of a Corretti, such answers could be given, especially as the press were no doubt nagging the desk for details.

She walked into the dark bedroom and took a moment for her eyes to accustom. Santo was deeply asleep—she could tell from the regular breathing and just the stillness in the room and the distinct lack of a smart comment from him.

'Santo?'

He rolled onto his stomach, pulled the pillow over his head.

'Santo!' She said it more firmly. 'It's two o'clock. The desk wants to know if you're checking out.'

'Did Alessandro call?'

'Nothing,' Ella said. 'Santo, it's time to get up.'

'Another hour...' came his sleepy voice, and then perhaps remembering it was Sunday after all and that he had taken up a lot of her time, he said the right thing. 'You go home.'

Then he said the wrong.

'Or—' he rolled now onto his side, a lazy smile on his sleepy mouth '—you can climb in.'

And she could go now, Ella knew. He could sort out the hotel himself. He was sober enough now to drive and she had loads to do—she was joining him on location in a couple of days and there was plenty to sort out. She turned and stood for a moment watching as he returned to sleep and then she left the bedroom.

Except it wasn't to collect her bag and leave.

Ella headed into the bathroom and stood there for a very long moment.

She trusted no one—it was absolutely safer that way. She didn't, thanks to a few months ago, even trust her own mother. And yet, in a bizarre way, she had an inkling of trust in Santo. He made no excuses and he never lied. Happily he put his hand up to claim his appalling reputation and somehow his honesty made her bold.

Because yes, Ella had wondered what it might be like to be made love to by Santo. Of course she had. After all, she had seen the most beautiful women shed hopeless tears over the man. Now, with one kiss, a little better she understood, but more than that, his kiss, his skill that had led her so close to willingness, it had made her curious.

Ella had never particularly enjoyed sex, possibly thanks to her poor choice of partners, for they had never ensured that she might, but she knew things would be different with Santo.

She just knew and, more than that, she wanted to know.

But she wouldn't cry over him.

Unlike the others Ella had no expectation to change him, knew that was never going to happen. She just wanted her sex lesson from the master, Ella told herself, wanted to go back to where his kiss had led.

It was for that reason she did as offered and changed her mind! There wasn't a romantic bone in her body— Ella knew that as she undid her blouse. She stood in the bathroom undressing and then headed into the bedroom and watched him sleeping for a moment. Then, naked, she looked at the warm bed and the man in it and, toes curling, she prepared to dive in.

She was cold, because as she joined him he told her she was.

He pulled her right into him and caught her feet between his calves and pressed his warm body to hers. For a moment she thought he had gone back to sleep, and then had a slight panic that he didn't even know who she was, because Santo was very used to not sleeping alone. He'd rung her once from a hotel bathroom, terrified to go back into the bedroom because he completely couldn't remember his date's name and had needed Ella to tell him.

She had to remember that.

'You feel better than you look,' Santo said, running warm hands over her breasts and then down to her hips, 'and you look amazing.'

Ella did not close her eyes. She would not give in to his effortless, well-used lines, would not allow herself to believe they were exclusive to her, even if he sounded as if he meant them.

'Am I dreaming, Ella?'

'No.'

'Because I won't be able to look at you if I am. This is going to be a really filthy dream....' He purred the words to her ear and she concentrated on the hands that were expert, that ran over and over her body till she was no longer cold and far more than warm. She felt the deep kiss on the back of her neck which would ensure her hair was worn down till late in the week as she was branded by Santo, and it felt good.

It felt good for Santo too.

That she had come to his bed was the most pleasant surprise. She was the strangest mix, direct at times and then so evasive, the one woman he had no idea about and yet he wanted to. 'What made you change your mind?' he persisted. 'Tell me so I know for next time.'

'There won't be a next time,' Ella said. 'Remember, we're writing off today.'

'Oh, there will be...' Santo would make sure of it. 'I've wanted you for so long.'

She squirmed as his mouth moved up and he kissed her ear. Ella tried to move away, but he clamped her down, his thigh over hers and trapping her still. His arm gripped her tight, his mouth unrelenting. It was horrible and wet, but he persisted till she found out she liked it, till her mouth was parting, till she wanted to crane her face to meet his mouth. He just kept on going and then stopped and taunted her wet, sensitive skin with words as his erection reared higher up the backs of her thighs.

'What made you change your mind?' he persisted, but still she did not answer, so he moved in with a different approach, 'I flew you to Roma.' It was wretched of him to bring it up here, horrible and mean, because he could feel her body burn in shame. 'I flew you first class and to a top hotel thinking you were going to the doctors when you were going to your interview....'

'I told you I wanted to make my own way,' she attempted. 'I was going to tell you. I thought I'd be called back for a second interview.' She stopped talking because he was kissing her neck and his fingers were pinching her nipples and none too gently either. There was this assault on her senses. He hurt a bit, but not enough, and his tongue was driving her crazy and her body wanted to turn, but still he pinned her, still he kept pausing to deliciously taunt her.

'What excuse would you have used for the second interview—would you have said you were having surgery this time?' His hand crept down. 'I was worried sick that you had to go all that way for a doctor's appointment.'

'Liar.'

'I was,' Santo insisted. 'I thought it was women's stuff, so I could not ask you.' His hand crept to a very womanly place. 'I thought you were being prodded and poked,' he said to her ear as he demonstrated and played doctor with his fingers. He was so indecent she thought she might cave there and then as intimately he explored her.

'Santo...' She didn't want her back to him. She wanted to turn to his mouth, wanted his kiss, wanted to see, but he held her firmly down. His fingers were inside, incredibly long fingers that thoroughly stroked, and if he carried on like that for much longer, Ella would be sobbing a confession of her own soon.

'Last night, with leech girl, I did consider I might be impotent.' He was licking the side of her breast, trying to get to her nipple as his hand brought her closer still.

'Please.' How could she be laughing and on the verge of coming, how could he make such a terrible topic so light?

'And now I worry that I might have *l'eiaculazione precoce*.' She was lying there, just giving in to her body for the first time and laughing, because he even made premature ejaculation sound sexy. 'So you understand when I say...' He released her then and her body, that had been desperate to turn, turned so naturally to him. It was just so wanton and readied by his hands, by his mouth, by his skin. As her mouth moved in to kiss him, he halted her, caught her chin with his hands and made sure she was looking as he spoke. 'Ella, in a moment I'm going to take you really fast,' he said. 'I mean, really fast, and then I'll spend the rest of the afternoon making up for it and doing you really slow.'

He leant over, his chest over her face, and patted the bedside table and then glanced around the room and cursed because his wallet was in his jacket in the bathroom. Then he smiled when Ella waggled a few packets she'd retrieved before coming to the bedroom.

Yes, it had been a calculated move.

'Good girl,' Santo said, thinking he'd never been more pleased to see a condom. And then, 'I'll do it...' because from the feel of her hand closing around his base and the lick on her lips as it did, it really could be over way to soon.

He dealt with things swiftly but Ella couldn't quite catch her breath as she saw firsthand the sight of Santo fully aroused. She reached out to touch him again, but he slapped her hand away. There was the tightness of anticipation in her throat because instead of kissing her, instead of joining her, he knelt between her legs and dragged her down the vast bed, till there were no pillows beneath her.

'I have been thinking about you for a very long time, since you turned up to be interviewed,' he admitted. He looked down at her naked beneath him and then smiled as he remembered that day. 'Your Italian was shocking.'

'So why did you hire me?'

'I wanted you.' Santo grinned. 'On sight I wanted you, and you can tell me tomorrow that you find that offensive. Right now I don't care.' And no, here in his bed, Ella didn't find it in the least offensive. She was just trying to remind herself that Santo was a master with women, knew how to say exactly the right thing, except she kept forgetting, found herself falling more and more to his corrupt charm. 'But if I had known how long you would make me wait...'

Just his words, just his want as he lifted her up by her buttocks and positioned her, had the blood flood to her groin. She had always thought him sexy, but there was this animal side to him, and it was a turn-on to watch the pleasure in him. His unrivalled passion had her shivering now to his words and had Ella wondering not just why, but how, she had waited. Being with Santo was just amazing, being in the spotlight of his gaze could so easily become addictive.

'Ella...' He didn't say any more for a moment, he didn't need to. Both their eyes closed as he squeezed into her, and she moaned at the excess, and then moaned again, because once he had filled her he was still for a second. Ella was desperate for movement, and her thighs were starting to shake. Then he stroked her slowly from the inside, a movement that had her squirming in pleasure. He opened his eyes and smiled down. 'You are worth the wait.'

And did he have to say such things, did he have to be so nice? Because for a second she believed he meant them. In that moment she had this vision of her near future—of her weeping and wailing and calling and being sent straight to his voice mail and being everything she had sworn she would not, because he was heartstoppingly amazing. He was way, way more than she had envisioned. Until now, nothing, not a single thing in her life, had ever felt this good.

'Buckle up.' Santo smiled a decadent smile.

'Sorry.'

'Cross your ankles, Ella.'

And in this, she rather liked having Santo as her boss. Ella did as she was told—locked her ankles together behind him—and he leant back into them, a small safety check before he shot her to the sky. There was no room for thoughts any more, no struggle to hold on, or anticipate regret. There was nothing other than the rapid thrust of him, the ferocity of Santo between her thighs as he jolted her out of sexual complacency, showed her how good it could be. She felt the first shudders of orgasm, felt the arch of her back in his hands, and she moaned her come as still he thrashed inside her.

'Come on, Ella...' He did not give her a moment to think, he just completely consumed her. He was holding on for dear life, when there was surely no need to, Ella thought, because she had already come, except she'd never been locked in orgasm with Santo. It was like falling through a trapdoor and then into another. He took her deeper into herself than she had ever been, deeper into them. This was supposed to be strictly sex, yet she was biting down not to shout his name. He moved her hips faster and then as his hands stilled her, as he bucked freely within, Ella was coming in a way she never had before, like lightning that strikes from the ground up. She didn't know where it began and ended. She was taut, writhing, frenzied and already crying over Santo as, satisfied by her surrender, he gave in then and pushed and pulsed within, dragging words out of Ella that made no sense even to her as she came again.

'Thank you...' The delicious assault on her senses didn't end as their bodies slowed down. He made it sound as if she'd just saved his life. He toppled onto her, was kissing her, his words dizzying. It wasn't over, it was a mere interlude. She was in his bed and going no-where, Santo was sure of it, because finally there was one good thing today and he wasn't about to let it go.

CHAPTER FIVE

Santo soon declared he was starving.

'There are some pastries out there...' Ella started, but then stopped. As if Santo would make do with stale pastries and tepid fruit juice—he was already reaching for the bedside phone.

'What do you want?' There was no consulting menus with Santo, Ella already knew that. He ordered and generally got whatever came first to mind.

'I don't mind.'

Santo ordered finger food and champagne, but unable to wait, he headed out and poured some fruit juice, looking out to the press below and sticking up one finger.

He'd checked his phone—still nothing from Alessandro. He flicked on his computer, more to see if there was any breaking news on his family, but he stood quiet for a moment, reading the email she had been sent, the last thing she'd been looking at before she joined him in his bed.

That was what had changed her mind.

He'd spent a long time wondering about Ella.

Too long thinking about how they'd be in bed.

And now he knew.

Except, unusually for Santo, he wanted to know more, a lot more.

He climbed back into bed and gave her a drink. When a little while later there was a knock at the door that declared their refreshment break was about to commence, unlike Santo, Ella couldn't just lie there as supplies were brought in, so she hid in the bathroom for a few moments, much to his amusement.

'You are such a prude.' Santo grinned as she walked back into the bedroom and he held open the sheet for her to climb in. 'And soon we will work on it, but first, I apologise—I am going to have to make some phone calls.' Of course the real world was waiting and she was more than used to Santo on the phone. All too often he wandered off, or stepped into another room, but this afternoon, privacy was somewhat discarded and they ate and drank champagne as he made a couple of rather terse phone calls to various family members. From the gist of things there was a lot of fallout from last night, which Santo confirmed when he hung up on the previous call and asked her to divert all calls unless it was his brother.

'Unless it is Alessandro I'm staying out of it.' He lay back and rested his hands above his head and looked up at the ceiling, examining yesterday's events a touch more calmly now. For once he wanted to talk about it with someone who wasn't family—not, of course, that he could tell Ella everything.

'You know we are going for the contract to renovate the docklands?'

'Sort of.' Ella, who was trying to decide between the sweetest figs she had ever tasted and the last of the chocolate-covered strawberries, looked over at him. Everything was so guarded with the Correttis and yet so intertwined. The docklands they were hoping to renovate was in fact being used for filming. She knew that the Correttis were hoping to breathe new life into the area and, naturally, bring a lot of money in.

'For me,' he said as she decided on a strawberry. Ella looked at him, aware almost that she was being tested.

She was.

She knelt over him and Santo took the food from her fingers. She watched as his teeth cracked the chocolate, as he took the last one, but at the last second he relented and pulled her head to his, let her have half. As she nibbled at the strawberry, she tasted, too, his mouth.

'I want to ring down for more strawberries.' Ella smiled as she spoke with her mouth full.

'There are figs—' he smiled '—and they are harder to separate and we don't want disturbing.' He looked at her glittering amber eyes and the pink on her cheeks that would soon be scalding again. He saw the new flare of arousal and he was about to pursue it, yet, surprising himself, he spoke. 'Salvatore, my grandfather, put it all in place before he died—that was the point of the wedding.'

'So it wasn't a love match between Alessandro and Alessia?' Ella asked. When Santo gave her a quizzical look Ella remembered she was in bed with a Corretti— and so she took it as a no!

'Battaglia has withdrawn his support.' What Santo didn't add was that Battaglia was now throwing his might behind Santo's half-brother, Angelo. There was just so much history in his family, so much feuding, and last night things had suddenly got a whole lot worse, not that he could tell her even half of it. 'Right now, all I want to concentrate on is the film.' Then he smiled over to her. 'And you.'

'I think you should save it for the film, Santo.' Ella wanted things left at the hotel checkout. She had no intention to wait till Santo got bored, yet as the conversation turned to the film, as his hands lazily wandered, as they fed each other figs with their mouths, reluctantly Ella admitted that there was no place she would rather be than here with him today.

'When did you first want to start directing?' He had dusted her breasts with chocolate powder and was now licking it off. The white sheets—like Santo, an absolute disgrace—but right now, Ella didn't care.

'Always,' Ella said.

'Always?' Santo checked. Ella thought for a moment, remembered being five or maybe six and just shutting herself in her room, closing off from the noises downstairs and making movies with her mind. Not just once, but over and over, changing the camera angle, concentrating on a scene, getting it so right. Any money she'd had went towards buying scripts, and later it was bliss to find them online. She was twenty-seven and had no experience, but she had been training for more than two decades now. 'It's what I've always wanted to do.'

'So why are you a PA?' Santo asked. 'You told me that was your passion when I interviewed you.' And he smiled as he remembered the very determined, extremely smart woman who had arrived in his office unannounced.

Then he licked around her areola till she was wet,

rather sticky, and she thought she might die if he didn't take it all in his mouth. 'You told me you took great pleasure ensuring your boss's life ran seamlessly.'

'I lied.' Ella smiled. 'As one does at interviews. Being your PA is my second passion in life, Santo.'

He could hear the wry note to her voice and it should have offended him. Why then did she make him smile? 'Third,' Santo said, because he wanted her again, but Ella was still talking about the film and she was lost to his hands for a moment, sitting up in bed with the sheet loosely wrapped around her, as if hiding herself from him as she spoke about the script.

It was a beautiful movie about a soldier going missing at war, presumed dead, and his wife turning to the soldier's best friend for comfort. Both drawing on each other in grief, resulting in her pregnancy, only to find out that her husband wasn't dead.

'It has to remain a love story,' Santo said. 'But really, there are a couple of parts where it doesn't gel for me,' Santo admitted. She loved that they could talk about movies, that they both shared this passion, because often Ella knew that she bored others with her observations and thoughts, but Santo was just as into it as her. 'I can't see how, if she loves him, she could just forget so soon.'

'She doesn't forget him though, not even for a minute.'

'If she can so easily sleep with someone else so soon after—' Santo was firm on this '—then he was not the one love of her life.' He frowned at her smile. 'What?'

'You're a fine one to talk.'

'I've never been in love,' Santo said. 'I don't even

know that it exists—this love-match you speak of.' He pondered it for a moment, scanned through his family history and shook his head. Then, as he opened up a little, Santo also convinced himself he was speaking with Ella for the sake of the film, rather than for his own peace of mind.

'My nonna said she fell straight in love with my grandfather.'

'See.'

'I never said it was returned. Salvatore loved power first—like my father.' He thought a moment more. 'My uncle, Benito…I thought he loved his first wife, but…' He gave a tight shrug. 'You know…' Ella watched as, for the first time she saw him pensive. 'Whether or not true love exists, in the film it has to be believable and that is going to be the struggle, because when Taylor and Vince make love the scenes are so passionate.'

'They don't make love,' Ella corrected. 'They have sex. She's grieving so badly and he comforts her.'

'A few days after the love of her life goes missing.' Santo gave a rueful smile. 'See now why we need a good actress?'

'Oh, yes.'

He looked over to her. 'Have you ever been in love, Ella?'

'No.' She looked over to him and smiled. 'I've been in lust.'

'I've seen.'

'But really,' Ella said, 'I'm not sure I'd want to be in love. I think it makes for less than sensible decisions.'

'Such as.'

Ella shrugged. 'I don't forgive and I never forget, which is a requirement apparently.'

'Apparently?'

'Well, from what I've seen.' She wasn't going to tell him about her family. She wanted nothing to dim this day, so she spoke about more casual acquaintances. 'I've got a friend back home and I've spent more hours watching her crying over the love of her life than I have seen her smiling. I've got another who—'

'What about your parents?' Santo interrupted her, realising just how little he knew about the woman who had been in his life for some considerable time now, by Santo's standards at least.

'Oh, I've seen a whole lot of forgiving and forgetting there too.' She gave him a grim smile, but refused to elaborate. 'So, all things considered, I think I'll stick with lust.'

Santo had no problem with that.

Or just a slight one, because he actually wanted to know a little more. But Santo was fast realising as he lay there that Ella was as skilled at deflecting personal conversations as he was. To prove his point, she returned to the discussion about the script.

'Do you think he forgives her?' Ella asked about the husband's return, about the kiss that would leave the audience hopefully reeling. It was the million-dollar question, the one he wanted the audience to be asking as they walked out of the theatre.

'I wouldn't.' Santo's response was decisive.

'Why not?' Ella challenged. Talking about film she was more animated than he had ever seen her, and for Santo, long may it continue because as she spoke, as her hands moved to make certain points, more and more of her left breast was being exposed.

'How can he?' Santo said. 'It's supposed to be the love of his life.' Then he gave a rueful smile, because of course there was no such thing as love. 'Perhaps,' he said, but he honestly didn't know. Really, he did want her opinion on this. 'What about you?'

'I don't know,' Ella admitted. 'I think that's the point of it though, that it's for the viewer to decide. I can't wait to see how Taylor will play it.'

'Nor me,' Santo admitted and they were quiet for a moment, sharing a similar vision, going over it in their minds—the script and a kiss that to the viewer must seem seamless but was actually going to be incredibly complicated to film. Ella had read the script over and over. Nothing was actually said at the end. It all came down to one kiss, an incredible reunion, relief mingled with fear as his hands roamed her body, as the soldier noticed the subtle changes, as he realised the love of his life had slept with someone else a matter of days after his supposed death.

This film had to work.

It had always been important to Santo, but never more so than now. With Alessandro gone, with the family name about to be smeared over the papers, for once there was a chance to prove himself, a chance to step out of his older brother's shadow and show that he wasn't a lightweight. He was dangerously close to telling Ella that.

He actually opened his mouth to. He looked at the woman in his bed and maybe that angry fist of Alessandro's had loosened something in his head, because for a second he thought about telling her what it was like growing up with Carlo as a father, how as the second son he had just been dismissed. He had even had the boardroom closed in his face once. Not one smile of approval from his father—not one. Not that Santo needed it, but there was something to prove now.

But even as he opened his mouth to tell her that, Santo changed his mind. There were things you didn't think about, let alone discuss with another, and he looked where the sheet had slipped and her breast was exposed. There was a welcome, most pleasing distraction from his race of dark thoughts.

'I think we need to sort out a few technicalities.' Santo smiled, and reaching for the bottle he topped up her glass.

'Oh, really?'

'I'm still struggling with the ending.'

'Which is why you are paying big bucks to someone like Taylor, to carry it off…' But her voice trailed off as she realised they were no longer actually discussing the film. Instead Santo had replaced the bottle then dipped into the ice bucket and pulled out a cube. She stared, fascinated, clutching on for dear life to her champagne glass, as his fingers approached her naked breast.

'The script reads that he notices the small changes to her breast…' He watched her bite down on her lip as he ran the ice cube around her nipple.

Her free hand went to move his, to stop him, but she wanted the full Santo experience. Instead she looked down at her nipple, tight and erect, and then, just as it was surely unbearable, she got the warm reprieve of his mouth. He sucked, gently at first and then deep, and just when it was too much, just when her body was begging for conclusion, his hand dipped back into the bucket for more ice.

'And realising that she might be pregnant—' Santo's voice was low as they worked through the script, as between words he kissed her '—his hand moves to her stomach...' And Ella's eyes screwed closed as in the film Taylor's must, but in Ella's case it was because his hand was full of ice. 'And still he kisses her,' Santo said, taking the dripping ice into his mouth and kissing her with a very cold tongue. 'Why would he still kiss her when he knows she has been unfaithful?' Santo lifted his head and asked her.

'Because when he stops kissing her, he knows they must talk and he doesn't want to know the truth.'

'Does he forgive her?' Santo asked. 'Does he end it?'

'He surely has to,' Ella said.

'Even though he loves her?' Santo checked.

'He cannot trust her,' Ella said.

'Too simple.' He was sucking on the ice and she watched the round, smoothed slivers as he ran them over her stomach.

She was so turned on, watching his fingers work the cubes down. She lifted her knees a little, blanched as he teased and intimately iced her then breathed as his tongue warmed and sucked a far more tender place than her breast.

And she was more than a willing participant. The sensations he delivered and the skill of his tongue were exquisite, and it was Ella sucking on ice cubes and passing them to him now.

For Santo, the feeling was incredible. He liked sex,

and a little play prior just to be nice, but if the clock stopped now, even without coming, this was the best sex he had had. He was just fascinated by her body, by the sighs and moans from her mouth, how if he put his tongue there her fingers tightened in his hair, and if he put it there, her hands sought her thighs and still she kept passing the ice.

'I always use…' He was pressing ice into her with his tongue and she thought she might die from the pleasure.

'I know,' Ella whimpered, locked between pleasure and pain.

'I want to try…'

'Please…' She was in this very strange place, where for the first time she could voice her want, did not have to be demure, be quiet, did not have to hold back what was on her mind. She had never opened up to another before, but she handed herself over to him now, if just for a while.

He climbed up her body and she was frozen deep on the inside and frenzied with heat at the surrounds. Her body, her skin, wet and cold from their games, sought the relief of him dry and warm now on top of her and he wrapped his arms under her.

'God, Ella…' He looked down, nervous at diving in as she begged him to hurry. Santo had never expected to be tentative his first time unsheathed, and she heard his shocked moan as he entered. 'I don't like it.' They were both shaking with laughter, with shock, with adventure, and then he moved a little more. 'Actually—' he rocked deeper and harder '—I've changed my mind.'

The friction warmed her, warmed him, till they were soaked and panting, and Santo was true to his word, had never made love unsheathed, but for this he willingly broke the rule. As she warmed to him he found new pleasures—the grip of her muscles, the increasing warmth. His promise to take forever, to do her slowly, was one he wanted to keep, for all he wanted was this.

'This morning I hated the day—' he was moving so fast within her now '—and now...' She couldn't understand what he was saying, she was too locked in her own thoughts. Then he was gracing her with Italian, but her brain didn't attempt to compute, because she felt her thighs starting to shake and this flood of warmth to her groin. But more than that, she was thrashing with her own thoughts, holding back her own words,

'Santo.' She considered for a brief second that the press outside must have got in, because lights were exploding in her head as if there were a thousand cameras aimed at them. She moaned and writhed and climaxed as Santo moved faster and it was bliss to come first, to just gloat from the podium and savour as he came a delicious last.

Santo was lost, feeling her pulse around him. He forced his own torture just so that he could feel each flicker and throb, and then gave in.

Ella watched his face contort and felt the pulse of his relief. Then, as if he might have been hit over the head, he collapsed onto her, the weight precious, the calm of sated. Santo lay there, his face in her hair that was spilled on the pillow, and he was almost nervous to look up.

It was the lack of condoms that had made it amazing, he told himself.

Or perhaps that he had wanted her for so long that made it all more intense?

'Santo?'

He went to move, assumed he was too heavy, except her hair was sliding beneath his face as she turned hers to his, and what Ella couldn't possibly know as his lips met hers was this was Santo's first kiss with meaning.

CHAPTER SIX

THEY ENDED UP checking out at four.

In the morning!

But, ever thoughtful, Santo left a huge tip for the maid.

The press were still convinced that Alessandro was in the hotel and so, instead of heading out there with soaking wet hair from the shower, Ella took a bit of time to dry it. She stood in bra and panties and put her make-up on and turned herself back into his PA again, but with Santo watching on.

'You like make-up,' he observed, watching her rouge her cheeks.

'Do I?' Ella answered, adding mascara and then moving to her lips, but Santo wasn't paying attention. He had taken out her concealer and was now standing behind her trying to cover up the mess he'd made of her neck. He looked amazing, wearing black jeans and black shirt and, with his eye a vivid purple, he looked sulking and rough. But there was a smile on the edge of his lips as he painted her neck.

'Do you want to borrow it?' Ella heard the slight edge to her own voice and fought to check it.

'No need.' He turned her round to face him. 'I never cover up my mistakes.'

And she'd have to see them.

It hit Ella then what she'd signed up for, understood all his ex-lovers' tears that she'd mopped. She had sworn she could handle just a little bit of Santo, but standing facing him, Ella knew enough about herself to know that already she wanted more. Yes, her notice should have been with immediate effect, because four weeks was way out of Santo's attention-span range.

As his mouth moved in to kiss her, as he hoisted her body to him, she could feel him dressed but indecent on her near-naked body and the effect of him made her nervous.

'No.' She said it too sharply. It came out too tense and quickly Ella qualified. 'I've just done my make-up.'

And in the world Santo inhabited, it was an entirely appropriate response, just his wasn't. 'I could turn you around then…'

He did just that. As he started to kiss her shoulder she watched his hands sliding over her stomach in the mirror and then she looked to her own eyes and saw her sudden panic, because he was going to be impossible to get over, because forever she would remember this.

And Ella didn't do sentiment.

'You've got a movie kicking off in a couple of hours and I want to go home.' She turned and smiled and she meant it. Ella put on her skirt and blouse and her shoes and made idle chit-chat, but she could hear blood whooshing in her ears, was fluttering in mild panic and didn't want him to see, didn't want to even give him a hint that he moved her.

Santo didn't seem to notice any difference in her. It was Santo who had changed, for this time as he faced her in the lift, he was a different man going down than up. Relaxed even as he headed out, not even bothering to scowl to the media, he saw her into the car, then drove towards Ella's villa. He needed no direction as he had dropped her off a couple of times before, but she had never asked him in and neither did she now. But Santo was having none of it.

'Make me coffee.' Santo yawned, because there was another drive ahead now to get to the run-down docklands where they were filming, only Ella wasn't joining him till Tuesday. 'And if you do…' He smiled. 'I will give you today off.'

'I was already taking it off anyway!' Ella said as he followed her into her villa. She was just a touch embarrassed—it was pretty sparse, just a small one-bedroom rental. As she headed into the kitchen to put the coffee pot on the stove Santo stayed in the lounge, looking at the few books she had and noticing they were all about directing.

Noticing, too, that, apart from that, there were no real clues to her.

He was very used to checking out women's homes—it was a fleeting game he played—but there was nothing to be learned about Ella here. Maybe it shouldn't have surprised him—she was only here temporarily after all—but there wasn't even a family photo above the fireplace.

And nothing much about her in her bathroom either, Santo noticed when he excused himself for a moment and shamelessly peered into her cabinets. He did make a mental note of her favourite scent and then smothered a smile, because he had been about to let Ella know, so she could order some, and flowers and jewellery too! Had she not been a woman she had just bedded, Ella would have been told later this morning that the works were needed for her new lover. For once, Santo wasn't feeling seedy after excess. Nope, there wasn't even the vague pang of guilt that happened all too often after an empty encounter.

'Coffee!' he heard her call from the kitchen. Santo glanced into her bedroom, saw the unmade bed and a bra on the floor. As exhausted as he was, as much as he needed to get to work, when he thought of her lying there calling him a bastard into her phone, he could easily have called to her to say to hell with the movie and that he wanted his coffee in bed.

Instead he headed back to the kitchen, watching as she poured the thick black coffee into two small cups and then sweetened them. She passed one to him and he took a grateful sip.

'For that—' he smiled '—you can turn your phone off till tomorrow.'

'And have you go crazy that I didn't pick up? I don't think so.'

'I mean it,' he said. 'Just have a day—I'll deal with anything that comes up. Turn your phone back on when you get there tomorrow.'

'I've got some things that need to be done....'

'Nothing that cannot wait. Do them tomorrow and then drive down—maybe get there in the evening. There won't be much action on set for a couple of days. It will all be setting up and getting to know the others.'

'You're sure?' Ella checked, because Santo was a pretty demanding boss, but she really was exhausted.

'Of course I'm sure,' Santo said. He watched her face closely when he spoke next. 'Unless you need to keep your phone on in case your family ring...'

'No.'

He took another sip of his coffee. She really gave nothing at all away.

'Your mother's Italian?' he checked. 'From where?' Santo asked, though he knew already from her dialect, but he wondered if she would share.

'Sicilian.'

'And your father?'

'He's Australian.'

And her eyes warned him that she would tell him no more than that, but he chose to ignore. 'Are they still together?'

'Why do you ask?'

'I just wondered...' Santo said. 'I was just asking about your family in the same way you asked about mine.'

And yes, Ella realised, she was being brittle and defensive when there was absolutely no need to be. It was a simple question after all. 'Yes—' she gave a tight smile '—they're still together.'

'Now,' Santo said, noticing her breathe out in relief as he changed the subject. But that soon faded when she found out to what he was changing it to. 'We need to speak about this job that you are considering taking....'

'No.' Firmly Ella shook her head. 'We've just spent the day and night in bed.'

'Which makes it a perfect time for talking.'

'For you, perhaps' was Ella's swift retort. 'I'll speak to you about this at work.'

'Ella, I don't want you taking that job.'

He didn't know how thin the ice was that he was skating on, because so many times her own father had used those very words to her mother.

'I choose where I work.'

'If you could just listen—'

'I mean it, Santo,' she interrupted. 'We will talk about this at work. You have a say in my career when we're there and that's the only place that you do.'

'You're being ridiculous.'

Not to Ella. Her mother had worked in a factory until Ella was born, but had given it up to help out in her father's shop.

Occasionally Ella could remember her mother asking her father if she could take an outside job—heaven knows they had needed the money—but her father had liked his wife close by, liked that she could speak little English, liked the lack of friends in her life.

'I don't care if you think I'm being ridiculous. I'll talk to you about this on Tuesday.'

'Can you hold off from responding to him till we've spoken though?'

'Santo!' Ella warned.

'Okay!' He wasn't at all used to being told no to anything but he conceded and gave her a very nice kiss on her mouth. 'Thank you—I never thought it possible, but you made yesterday a good one.'

'And you.' She smiled back at him, conflicted. She wanted him gone, yet she did not want to let him go, did not want him heading off to the film set without her. She could feel little snaps of doubt biting at her, because, really, Ella wasn't so sure that she could handle this. Santo was big league—no matter how much she told herself that this wasn't going to hurt, there was the sensible part that was starting to realise that it was.

Any day soon.

She looked into his eyes, perhaps for the last time like this, because with Santo's track records he could be in Taylor's arms tonight.

'Good luck with the first day of shooting.'

'I'll need it...' Santo rolled his eyes.

'What are you going to say to Taylor about the photos?'

'What's the point saying anything?' Santo shrugged. 'I told her to behave. I told her how much the film was relying on her to stay out of trouble. Really, it might be easier to just stitch her knees together.'

Ella laughed as she said goodbye to him, but her heart wasn't in it—because even with her knees stitched together Taylor was still breathtakingly beautiful, and Ella wouldn't put it past Santo to be ringing her at midnight with an urgent call for scissors!

Except, Ella remembered, she was turning off her phone.

It was bliss to climb into bed and to know that nothing would disturb her, except she hadn't counted on her thoughts. The panic that had gripped her in the hotel bathroom was back now.

It wasn't just sex.

She lay staring up at the ceiling, still trying to tell herself that it was, that she could do this. Ella had long since guarded her heart well, so she certainly wasn't going to start holding out hope for Santo. She smiled at the very thought of him reformed, but then it faded, because even if the reformed Santo came tied up with a bow she'd never be able to trust him.

Ella slept well into late afternoon, but of course as soon as she woke she checked her phone—presuming, because she knew how he operated, there would be an awful lot of calls and endless texts from Santo. To be in his spotlight was intense.

Nothing.

She checked and checked again, trying to batten down her disappointment before it properly took hold. Surely she should be pleased he hadn't bombarded her, except...yes, the high she had been floating on was starting to disperse. Without her propping Santo up, there were no flowers arriving at her door bearing cards filled with overused sentiments. Ella even managed a wry smile as she recalled one of their recent conversations.

'What should I put?' She'd checked when he'd told her to send some flowers.

'You decide.'

He'd clearly had second thoughts about leaving this particular note to Ella, because he'd buzzed her a few minutes later. 'What did you put?'

Ella had sighed before replying. "I enjoyed our weekend. You were amazing. Santo."

'No, that's the flowers she should be sending me.' He thought for a moment. 'Don't worry about flowers, just some jewellery, sapphire.'

'She's got blue eyes then, has she?'

Yes, she knew him too well.

Stop it, Ella, she told herself as she set about packing for the shoot, reminding herself that she wasn't going to let Santo upset her, that she had gone into this with her eyes wide open. Then, refusing to heed Santo's advice on her career, she replied to Luigi and accepted the job and then wrote out her resignation—because whatever happened now between her and Santo, she wouldn't be working for him for much longer.

She got through the night without a single word from Santo and long into the next day, running the million errands a wild weekend in Santo Corretti's life generated. It was actually late evening by the time she finally pulled up at the boutique hotel, close to where filming would take place. The drive should have been a pleasant one—the scenery was stunning after all, the traffic light—but she passed a few signs for her mother's village, and though the area where they were filming wasn't where her mother had come from, it was closer than Ella felt comfortable with. Stepping out of her car, there was a knot of unease in her stomach. It was her mum's birthday in a few days and she'd have no choice but to ring her. If her mother found out just how close she was to her village, it would be terribly awkward not to visit her aunts.

Rude, in fact.

There were certain rules in all families, but none more so than a Sicilian one, Ella thought as she walked through the glass revolving doors.

There was a faded beauty to the hotel, a quiet elegance to it, and the staff were formal but friendly. Once checked in, Ella headed to the gated lifts, blinking as Taylor Carmichael stepped out. She was wearing huge dark glasses, and Ella gave a shy smile of greeting, but of course, Taylor had no idea she worked for Santo and naturally she was ignored.

Still, it was so exciting to glimpse such a celebrity, and to think that tomorrow she might get a chance to watch her acting and the movie Ella loved start to unfold.

Ella found her room and swiped the card but frowned as the door opened. The hotel was gorgeous, but this room was seriously stunning. Ella stood a moment. The French windows were open to a large private terrace, taking every advantage of the aquamarine sea, and surely she would ask for the rich heavy drapes to be left open at night, just to drink it all in. Ella looked at the antique furniture and huge gilded mirrors and wondered if she'd been upgraded. There were vases of fresh flowers, even champagne chilling in a bucket, and she blushed at the memory of the other night, a smile playing on her lips as she did so. Realising now that this was the work of Santo, she was touched that he had been so thoughtful. But it faded as she heard Santo talking from the bedroom and, realising the mistake, she walked over and picked up the internal phone.

'Ella…' Santo came out then. 'At last, you're here.'

'I am!' She was suddenly awkward, embarrassed that she had thought he'd ordered flowers and champagne for her room. 'There's been a mistake at reception. I think they thought I was sharing with you.' She rolled her eyes. 'I spoke in Italian when I made the booking. I must remember not to in future.'

'There's no mistake.' Santo smiled. 'I asked them to

send you to here. I thought we could have dinner, talk—there has been so much happening....'

'You can't just move me in.'

'I am not just moving you in,' Santo said.

'So where's my room?' Ella asked.

'Ella, we will be working fifteen-hour days...or at least I hope that we will.'

'Sorry?'

'The director quit.'

Ella's mouth gaped open, her living arrangements temporarily forgotten.

'He quit?'

'He gave ultimatums. I do not like ultimatums.'

Ella had seen him clash with directors now and then, but to lose one on the first day of filming...it must have been a pretty spectacular row. She asked him what had happened.

'It's finished with now.' Santo shrugged. He was never one to go over the past, as always he moved easily on. 'I have been chasing around trying to think of who would be best to direct the movie, and who is available too, but I think that finally it is sorted.' He was pouring champagne and there was a small flurry in Ella's stomach as he handed her the glass that had bubbles rising in it, like the sudden hope that for Ella flared. 'I have found someone good, someone who I think shares my vision, who really is keen to bring out the very best in Taylor.' He smiled at Ella and she gave a tentative one back. 'Tomorrow we have a new director starting, Rafaele Beninato.'

'Rafaele Beninato?' He must have heard the disappointment in her voice. She simply was too upset to hide it. Because of the champagne, the smile, the conversations they had had about the movie, the visions they had shared, Ella really had, for a blind, stupid moment, thought that Santo was going to give the role to her.

'Ella…' Not only did Santo hear her disappointment, he saw the burn of her cheeks. 'You didn't think—'

'No.' She was embarrassed to admit that yes, she had thought he might consider her. After all, this was a major movie they were talking about, as if he was going to trust it to her. But then Ella was suddenly angry too, that he hadn't. 'It's that you didn't think! That you didn't even consider me for the role.'

'How could I?' He was incredulous. 'Ella, you have no experience whatsoever.'

'No!' She was beyond hurt now. They had lain in bed just yesterday, acting it out, going over scenes. But clearly, not once had it entered his head that she might make a good director.

Yes, it hurt.

'Santo, I love that movie. I have gone over and over the script. I know it inside out. I know exactly what's needed.' She put down her glass, missing the coaster, her feelings raw, because while his words made perfect sense, were completely logical, Ella wasn't thinking logically right now. 'I'm going to change the booking.…' She just wanted away before she said too much, wanted to think, and she couldn't with Santo so close. Ella, who never cried, was dangerously close to doing so as she picked up the phone and asked that the booking be reverted back to the one she had made. She told the receptionist that she'd come down and get the key now.

'So you're storming out because you didn't get the part?'

'No!' Ella snapped. 'I was leaving already. That's the whole point of separate rooms, Santo—there's somewhere to go when you row!'

Ella's bags arrived then and she quickly diverted them, but there was her room key to collect and it took forever until she was finally alone. Ella attempted to gather her thoughts, but even that didn't last for long, because in no time at all, Santo was rapping on her door, refusing to budge till she let him in.

'You want it both ways.' It was Santo who was angry and aggrieved now. 'You insist that we keep work separate—you make this great song and dance as to how we cannot work and sleep together, that we are to keep things professional at work, yet when it suits you want all the favours of being my lover.'

'That's not true.'

'Yes.' Santo stood firm. 'It is true. You want it both ways,' Santo said. 'I want it only one. I am myself now and in the bedroom, but at work I make the best decisions for my movies.' She heard the passion then, the absolute single-mindedness that made him so brilliant. 'When I am at work I choose only the best for my films and I make decisions with my head only at all times, and if you think I am going to hand over a director's role because we have good sex, then you are the one who has an issue, not me.'

'I wanted that role long before yesterday.'

'And I did not consider you for that role long before yesterday too, because the fact is, Ella, you have no experience.'

'Because you won't give me any.'

'When a suitable vacancy comes up, it will be yours, but the world is not waiting for you to debut, Ella. You have to earn your stripes in the industry to be respected and not in the bedroom.'

She wanted to slap him, his words burnt so, but instead Ella stood with her face scalding, because what he was saying was true and he hadn't finished yet. 'So, to reiterate, I enjoyed our time together. I hoped to take things further today. I hoped to share a meal, to talk, to make love. But instead, because you cannot manage to separate work from the bedroom, instead we sleep alone.'

'I'm handing in my notice....'

'More fool you,' Santo said. 'Go work for Luigi, go let him dangle you the promise, and you will find out I am not such a bastard after all. And at least you enjoy sleeping with me.'

'Luigi is nothing like that,' Ella flared. 'He's a brilliant director and he's keen to have a willing assistant—'

'Hey,' Santo interrupted, 'you know when people wait while their potential employers ring for references. I often wonder why don't the potential employees do the same? Why don't they take a little while to find out what they are getting into before they jump?'

'I wish to hell I had.'

'No.' So swift was his retort. 'You knew exactly what you were getting into. As I said, I don't hide my supposed mistakes and I don't expect favours and neither do I give them for sex.' For a man who appeared to have no morals, he stood there and proved otherwise. 'For all the bastard you seem to think I am, think carefully,

Ella—because your job has never depended on sleeping with me and it still doesn't. I know how to close the bedroom door and carry on with my work.'

Her back was to the wall, and not just literally, because he was right.

'How much notice are you giving?'

'Four weeks.'

'Fine,' Santo said. 'Ring the agency tomorrow for your replacement, see if you can get someone who can start ASAP so that you can train them up. And, this time, can you tell them I want someone fully fluent in Italian, please?'

How that stung but she refused to jump.

'Anything else?'

'With a lot of experience.'

'Good looking too?' Ella jeered.

'I would hope so,' Santo said without contrition. 'And preferably without too many hang-ups and issues.'

'You can go on your own dating sites....'

'I don't go on dating sites,' Santo said. 'I don't need to, and anyway, I don't have time,' he retorted. 'I want someone who is good at their job, who is pleasing to the eye, and someone who doesn't pin everything on what happens between the sheets.' And with that he walked out and slammed the door.

He was right.

Ella sat shaking on the bed.

Her disappointment was on a professional level but it was personal too.

It was she who couldn't separate things, but of course, with Santo, she'd never been able to.

Ella admitted it herself then—every woman he'd

dated, every time he'd crooned into the phone to his latest lover as she drove, she'd had bile black and hissing in her stomach and it had felt like a personal slight.

She had known what she was getting into but had completely ignored it, just to have the refuge of work. Had chosen to keep her days busy when she should have lain on a beach and somehow healed from all that had happened with her father. When she should perhaps have curled up and hid for a while to process things, instead she'd insisted to herself she was fine and had looked for a job, had ignored what now she could not.

A hotel room was not a nice place to be gripped by panic and unlike Santo's there was no private terrace, just shuttered windows which Ella flung open and gulped in night air. She wanted to ring home, wanted to scream, wanted to run to Santo and batter down his door, for she could not stand to be alone with her thoughts.

She could not bear to remember the feel of her father's fist in her face and the screams and shouts from her mum and the feeling of being twenty-seven and feeling as if she were six.

Except right now she was doing exactly that.

Remembering every horrible moment, every terrible feeling, crying and sobbing for the first time since it happened, reliving the nightmare when she didn't want to…

…and in a hotel room alone.

CHAPTER SEVEN

FOR THE FIRST time since she had started working for him, Ella wondered if she could face breakfast with Santo and going through his diary. They always started the week like that, and as she'd had yesterday off, it would be assumed she would meet him in the hotel restaurant at 6:00 a.m., as they did when on location.

Ella stood in front of the mirror after a very sleepless night. A cool shower had done little to reduce her swollen eyelids and the tip of her nose was bright red.

She looked like a woman who had spent the night crying.

Except she hadn't, as Santo would no doubt assume, been crying over him—it was the issues that he had alluded to that had finally made her break down.

It had been six months without tears.

Six months of telling herself that she was strong, that she would not let what her father had done affect her, would not let his fists bruise her soul.

But they had.

It wasn't just the beating that had left its mark.

It was the years that had.

Years of watching her mother suffer, years of walking on eggshells so as not to upset him, years of scrimping and saving to afford a home where she could take her mother away from him.

Ella was in danger of crying again, so she chose not to think about that awful day. Instead she attempted magic with a make-up brush, but nothing was really going to work. So, once dressed, it was Ella who donned huge sunglasses this morning and took the elevator down, fervently hoping that Santo would be polite and pretend not to notice the state of her face.

'Jesus!' He stood up as she approached the table. Of course he looked immaculate and well rested. Because it was Santo he promptly took her glasses off—he was just so bloody Italian—and wrapped her in his arms. 'Sorry, baby…'

'Stop it.'

'I went too far.' He was talking into her ear, slowing her heart that had been beating frantically all night. 'Hire someone ugly—' she felt tears fill her eyes at his attempt to help '—a man, I don't care.'

'Santo.' She pushed him off a little, took a seat. 'I wasn't crying about that.' A waiter poured her coffee and Santo sweetened it for her. She took a drink of it and wished he wasn't being so nice, because it would be so easy to again break down. 'I've got stuff going on. You were right.'

'Of course I was right,' Santo said. 'About what?'

'You know…' God, but she hated the word. 'Issues…'

And where most men would run Santo was over in a flash. He moved his chair right beside her and wrapped an arm around. 'Tell me.'

'No!' She did not want his arm, did not want a man who was so comfortable in his own skin that he could sit in a restaurant and not care who saw, nor one who thought she could discuss such things.

'I'll tell you mine.'

'No.' She was not going to let him make her smile.

'I've got hundreds of them,' Santo said, and yes, he made her smile. Then he was terribly kind. 'But right now, my main issue is you.'

'We've got to head over to the set.'

'I'll say when we go.'

'I can't talk about it.'

'You could.'

'No.' Ella shook her head. She didn't have to explain her choices to him, except she found herself trying to. 'You don't talk about things you don't want to, you don't discuss your family.'

'You know my family are...' He didn't finish and she looked over, watched his hand move to the collar of his shirt as he struggled to come up with a suitable answer, but Ella found it for him.

'You're a Corretti,' Ella said. 'So your troubles are far darker and far more serious than mine could ever be.'

'Yes.'

'I was being sarcastic, Santo.'

'I know,' he said. 'And so was I, but what I'm trying to tell you is that there is little that hasn't happened in my family. My nonno, Salvatore, started with nothing and died one of Sicily's most powerful men, so yes, there are things that I cannot talk about. His sons—my father, Carlo, and his brother, Benito...' Santo stopped then. 'You know what they say about loose lips...'

'Speaking of ships...' She went to tell him about an arrangement for the film but he stopped her.

'Don't change the subject.'

'I am changing it, Santo, because in being so open about your family and issues, you've told me precisely nothing.'

'I'm trying to let you know that you can tell me if you want to,' he said. 'And if you can't, that is fine, but you are never to spend a night like that alone again when I am a short elevator ride away.'

'Santo…' Someone was calling out to him, telling him it was time to head off, but he called over his shoulder that he would catch up with them there.

'Do you understand me?'

'Sometimes it's better to be on your own.'

'You prefer what you went through last night to making love with me?' He kissed her temple. 'Then you are mad.'

'Sex isn't the answer to everything.'

'It's a good one though,' he said. 'It works very well for me. But if you want to continue with your sex strike, still we can talk.' He stood, offered his hand. 'Come on, we can walk to the set.'

'It will take too long.'

'They can wait for me,' Santo said with all the arrogance of someone who knew that the world would. He handed her back her sunglasses as they stepped outside and he was the nicest company, pointed out villages as they walked down the hillside.

'My mum's from there,' Ella said, wondering if it was being here that had upset her and perhaps brought it all to a head. 'I've got aunts there.'

'Are you going to visit?'

'Maybe after we finish shooting.'

'Don't tell them you work for me then,' he nudged. 'They will warn you.'

'I already know your reputation.'

'Not me,' Santo said, 'my family.' He pointed yonder. 'My nonna lives over there. There is a lot of history, a lot of enemies have been made. Ours is not always a good name.' He gave her another nudge. 'Issues.' But this time it didn't make her smile and for the first time Santo knew he couldn't just joke his way out of things, that her silence was perhaps a demand for something more, something he had never given. Except he looked at her swollen lips and thought of her eyes puffy behind the glasses. If he wanted more, then Santo realised he had first to give.

'My father and his brother were killed in a ware-house fire.' He wasn't telling her any great secret. It had been the talk of Sicily then and still was at times. 'That is when my grandfather divided everything up.'

'When the warring started?'

'Oh, it started long before that,' Santo admitted. 'My father and Benito were always rivals, Salvatore saw to that.'

'You call him Salvatore?'

'I call him both,' Santo said. 'You don't really sit through business meetings saying Papà and Nonno.'

'I guess.'

'It's got worse since he divided things up. Once a year we put on an act and are civil.' He saw her frown, explained just a little bit more. 'The family gets together at my nonna's each year for her birthday—the only thing we all agree on is that we adore her, and we call a truce for one day, but after that, it's gloves off again. These next few weeks…'

Santo shook his head. He simply never went there, not even with himself, and really, there wasn't time to now. There was a movie to be made after all. Except Santo found himself standing on a hillside and looking out to the docklands and the sea beyond, thinking how black it had all seemed on Sunday, the hell he had felt in a hotel room, except Ella had been there for him, had turned that day around. He wished last night she had let him do the same, wanted her to open up to him, so for her he broke his unspoken rule.

'My grandfather played his sons off against the other. He taught them from the start that to get on you had to be ruthless.' He looked at Ella. 'So they were. When his health got worse he divided things up. Benito he put in charge of the hotel empire, and my father, Carlo, media. Now though, if we want the proposal to redevelop the docklands to go through, we need to pull together.' He gave a wry grin. 'I can't see it happening. Angelo is—'

'Angelo?'

'My half-brother.'

'You never said.'

'I never do.' He looked down the hill. 'He has bought some of the houses here. This is supposed to be our development, but now Battaglia is throwing his weight behind Angelo.'

'Because the marriage didn't go ahead?'

'Because of so many things.'

'Does it matter?' Ella ventured. 'I mean, it's just one project.'

'It matters,' Santo said, and in that he wasn't going

to go into detail, wasn't about to tell her that the Cor-retti empire was crumbling around them. It wasn't so much that he didn't trust her—he could not bear to admit it to himself.

'Right now, I need to concentrate on this movie, but first...' He pulled her into his arms and took her glasses off again, and kissed her very nicely, strangely ten-derly. It made her want to cry, because she understood perfectly now her predecessors' tears and rantings. It wasn't just the sex—Santo Corretti was the whole pack-age. How cold and lonely would the world be after him.

And then, when his phone started begging for the producer to please arrive on set, there was no choice but to get moving.

They arrived at the docklands. It was rough and worn down, but Santo told her that with some money thrown at it, it would one day again be so beautiful. 'The town is dying,' Santo said, 'but if the tourists found it, if the people came back...' There were locals all gathered to watch the activity. 'See...' Santo said. 'That café has not been open for years, but now, today, it is. That is the sort of thing this film could do, and maybe it would have the people associate the Corretti name with what it can do in the future, not ways of old....' Then he stopped talking about family. 'Will you do one thing for me?' Santo asked before he got to work. 'Will you check out Luigi before you accept the job?'

'I've already accepted it.'

To his credit, Santo said nothing, not that he had much chance to. He was in a lot of demand and Ella took a seat and started working. Or trying to work, more often than not she found herself peering over her

computer, frowning at a couple of Rafaele's suggestions, because they weren't interpretations Ella would
have considered.

Still, Rafaele was the expert, Ella told herself, determined to put pride aside and to learn from him.

'Are you okay?' Ella blinked in surprise a little while
later to the sight of Santo handing her a coffee.

'Better,' Ella said.

'Because if you being here is a bit much, I don't
need you.' He winced. 'That came out so wrong—what
I meant...'

'I know what you meant.' Ella smiled, touched that
he seemed to realise that last night had been about so
much more than their exchange of words. 'How's it
going?'

Santo grimaced. 'Vince just lost his temper. I don't
know. It's early days, I guess.'

She sipped on her coffee, but after a moment or so
she decided to take him up on his offer. 'If you're sure
you don't need me I might go and get some work done
in the hotel.'

'Sure,' Santo said. 'I'll call if I need anything.'

It was safer to be alone right now—she simply
daren't get closer to him. He'd been open, far more
open about his family than Ella had expected him to
be and, as nice as it had been to talk, on reflection it
disarmed her. Sex she could handle—it was the rest
that terrified her so. Holding that thought once back in
her room Ella contacted the agency that had first sent
her to Santo. She spent most of the day going through
résumés as well as confirming the docking times for
the ship which was going to be a huge part of the film

set. Ella did a few phone and online interviews, until she had narrowed it down to two. Then she checked her own emails, frowning a little at the response from Luigi, who was, he said, delighted to give her this opportunity and that he was looking forward to seeing her when she came to Rome, that they must have dinner as soon as she got there.

Of course Luigi would want to take her out to dinner and go over things before filming started. It was dinner, Ella told herself as she headed down to the restaurant to have dinner herself with Santo.

'Better?' Santo checked, standing briefly as she walked over.

'Much.'

And then there was no more personal talk, because there was actually an awful lot of work to discuss, especially now that they had started shooting. They worked their way through most of it, even the rather more delicate stuff.

'Her name is Marianna Tonito.' Ella brought him up to speed on her potential replacements. 'She's worked for two movie producers and one film star, so she has loads of experience. I spoke to the agency and then I spoke to her. She seems very...' Ella struggled for the right word—knowledgeable, competent, confident, all applied, and thanks to the magic of Skype, Ella knew that Marianna was also terribly, terribly sexy. 'Suitable' was the word Ella settled for, though she knew that she was handing inevitable heartbreak over as she passed Santo the résumé, but Marianna was in fact the perfect person for this role.

'When can she start?'

'Immediately.'

Santo frowned. 'How can she be so good if she is so available?'

'I checked all that.' Ella had thought exactly the same. 'She's still working, much the same as me—actually training up her replacement now, at her boss's wife's request.'

Ella saw the slight raise of one eyebrow. 'Are there any other candidates?'

Ella handed him the second résumé. Santo tried, he really did, to keep his expression bland—so much so that Ella had to suppress a smile. 'He seems to have a lot of experience.'

'He does,' Santo said carefully. 'And perhaps things would be a little less complicated.' He glanced over to Ella, as if to check her thoughts, but she refused to give them. 'How soon can he start?'

'Paulo has already given his notice. He's in Singapore now with his current boss, but should be back in Italy in the next couple of days, though he wants to take two weeks off before he starts a new job.'

'Fly them both over for an interview.' He could feel this huge sulk unfurling. He did not want her gone. It was all so unnecessary to Santo, and certainly he did not want her working for Luigi. 'You haven't given your notice in writing.'

She went into her huge handbag and took it out. 'I meant to give it to you last night.'

He didn't take it.

'File it.'

'Fine.'

'In the shredder.'

'I'll email you a copy before I do,' Ella said. 'Anything else?'

'I need to change the ship date.'

Ella blinked. Surely he wasn't talking about the ship date. It had taken her forever to organise—ships sailing into the sunrise generally did!

'I need you to make it for two days later.'

'Santo…' Ella drew a long breath. It was just the sort of request she'd come to expect from him, just the usual impossible ask that with one look he expected her to fix. 'There are three hundred extras booked.'

'You think that I don't know that?' Santo responded. 'But the fact is we lost a day's filming yesterday and things haven't exactly gone well today.' She sat quiet for a moment as he voiced it. No, things hadn't gone well. All the hope and excitement that had greeted them this morning had slowly dispersed throughout the morning, and from the whispers Ella was hearing, after she had left things had gone from bad to worse. 'I think I might have made a mistake.'

He didn't actually say it, but Ella knew that he was talking about Taylor. She hadn't exactly shone today, but Ella could see it wasn't her acting that was the problem. Though it would sound like sour grapes if Ella suggested that it was the director who was the issue.

'Things might improve tomorrow,' Ella attempted. 'It was never going to be perfect the first day of filming.'

'I know. But for now just sort out the ship and the extras. We're going to need more time.'

'I'll see what I can to…' Her voice trailed off as his phone bleeped the text. She watched relief flood his face.

'Alessandro?'

'Thank God,' Santo said, reading the text. Ella found herself wishing he'd tell her what his brother had said. She wanted more into his life and was having terrible trouble dealing with that. 'So we're done?'

Ella nodded.

'Did you want another drink?' he offered.

'No, thanks.'

'Did you want to talk?'

'We're up at five tomorrow.'

'Fine.' He was curt—it had been a hell of a day and not a particularly good last night and Santo would love to happily screw his way out of it, but he wasn't going to beg.

He didn't understand her.

But he'd tried to.

'You'd really rather be alone than be with me.'

Yes, Ella thought, because it was safer to be alone tonight. In his bed she'd be telling him she loved him or something ridiculous, which wouldn't cause a remote problem for Santo, Ella knew. He was more than used to hearing that.

It just caused a huge problem for Ella. She simply didn't want to love anyone, didn't want her heart out there in harm's way, and she was already scrambling to take it back.

''Night, Santo,' she said, because it was far safer too.

''Night, Ella.'

CHAPTER EIGHT

SHE WAS UNABLE to get hold of Paulo for a couple of days, but when Ella did he was delighted to hear from her.

But trying to arrange an interview proved a little difficult. 'What about next Sunday?' Ella peered at the diary, then changed her mind. If they changed the shipping dates, it would be the final day of filming and there would be three hundred extras milling around and the set would be crazy. 'Let me sort out things this end and then I'll get back to you.'

'No problem.' He was just so funny and nice and keen to work for Santo, and he told Ella that he was happy now to take just one week off between jobs. 'Even no time off, but don't tell him that yet—I would love to work for Santo,' Paulo said. 'I have heard so many good things.' He laughed then and so did Ella. 'Lots of terrible things too—the whole family, really. They're a PR nightmare. I assume you've seen the papers this morning?'

'You really don't expect me to discuss that!' Ella smiled, because there were tales of infidelity and missing grooms and illegitimacies. It was Santo's mother, Carmela, who was taking up the news today. She was an exceptionally cold woman, one who had been more interested, the newspaper article read, in her designer suits than being a mother to her children. Even if Santo knew that already, he was surely reeling from the news that had just broken of his mother's most illicit affair.

She turned her attention back to Paulo. They really weren't gossiping. Ella had asked him questions about his employer, liking the fact that though Paulo chatted away, he told her nothing. 'There is an awful lot of discretion required for this role.'

'Of course.'

'Even with Santo—though you work alongside him, really, you won't have a clue half the time what is going on. He especially doesn't discuss his family.'

'I would never expect a Corretti to,' Paulo said. 'I am Sicilian, I know.'

Marianna was nowhere near as accommodating or as pleasant to speak to as Paulo.

Most annoyingly, Marianna insisted on speaking in English. God, the Italians were so good at delivering a snub when they wanted to, but Ella took it nowhere near as well as she did when it was Santo. It was even harder to pin her for an interview time than it had been with Paulo.

'I'll arrange transport for you if you can just give me a suitable date.' Ella did her best to keep her voice even. 'Santo really would like to get this organised as soon as possible, so if you could let me know when you're available, I'll try to sort things out with him.'

'I'll arrange my own transport,' Marianna said. 'You can reimburse.' Ella held on to her breath. Really, she felt rather more as if she were the one being interviewed, as if she was Marianna's assistant. She tried to remember that this was the sort of person best for the job—someone brash and confident, someone who would be able to reschedule a ship at five minutes' notice and deal with all the drama Santo generated. There was certainly no off-the-record chats with Marianna. In fact, she wanted to speak only with the man himself.

'I will look in my diary and see when I am available. Perhaps if I speak directly with Santo...'

'Santo is busy with filming at the moment,' Ella said. 'I arrange his diary.' And she heard the note of possession in her own voice and tried to stifle it. 'If we can organise a mutual time that would be great, but there are several applicants and Santo is very busy.'

'I'll be in touch.' It was Marianna who rang off.

Still, it was a minor triviality and not one she would worry Santo with, because the filming was going from bad to worse and, as the days progressed and the filming didn't, his mood darkened. The crew were putting in incredibly long hours but it was seemingly all going backwards. Still, Ella had more on her mind than Santo. It was the day she had been dreading for weeks—her mother's birthday—and later she needed to ring her.

And say what?

Ella tried not to think about it. Instead she responded to a couple of texts from Santo, who was already on set, and then sorted out some of his overnight correspondence.

The second it was 9:00 a.m., she started on the endless phone calls to sort out the extras and ship, and then it was time to head for the set.

She could feel the tension on set as she approached.

Santo had been right to reschedule the ship scene. There was no way they would have been ready otherwise.

'Where's Vince?' someone called.

'Sulking in his trailer.' Santo scowled back.

She looked to where Rafaele was placing all the actors, and then glanced over to Santo. There was a muscle jumping in his cheek as he watched the placement. 'What the hell is he doing?'

Ella said nothing—it wasn't her place to—but how she would have loved to get in and change things. Rafaele had Vince walking along the docklands where he would come across Taylor crying and stand watching her for a long moment before making his way over.

It didn't work.

The characters weren't supposed to even like each other and it just made Vince look opportunistic, especially when Rafaele asked him to put more purpose in his stride.

'Yep…' Santo gritted. 'March over there, why don't you…' He turned his head to Ella. 'Is Rafaele reading the same script as you and me?' Ella said nothing, just watched in silence as, yet again, the make-up team were called on to touch up Taylor's make-up.

'This is a disaster,' hissed Santo.

Again Ella said nothing.

But absolutely he was right.

Over and over they watched as Taylor cried on cue, and then, over and over, Rafaele called for her to do it again.

'It's too much,' Santo said, and Ella stayed silent, knowing Santo wasn't stressing about the pressure on Taylor. It was that there was far too much going on in the scene that was the problem. This particular scene was to be combined with a flashback of her receiving the news that her lover had died. It was supposed to portray the devastated heroine staring out to sea and breaking down as she realised her lover would never return.

'Action,' Rafaele called, and Ella watched as again Taylor broke down. Vince was being filmed too, from the rear first, watching her from a distance, then walking across the docklands towards her. It was at the end of this scene their grief and passion would ignite.

'First her face—' Santo was incensed '—then the beach, then back to her face, and now Vince.'

Santo was right. Vince was just bombarding the scene. Ella could see what was needed, could actually see it before her eyes. Taylor was acting beautifully. It was an Italian shot that was needed—an extreme close-up of her eyes with the ocean reflected in them and then turning as Vince joined her side.

God, she could see it.

'It's going to be like watching tennis,' Santo moaned.

Still Ella said nothing, just watched as a very tense Taylor flounced off. Finally Rafaele told everyone to break for lunch.

'What do you think?'

An ironic smile twisted her lips, that he had the audacity to ask her.

'Come on, Ella, say what you're thinking.'

'That I need your signature to transfer some funds for the extras....'

'I meant about this scene.'

'I'm your PA,' Ella said. 'You declined directing advice from me.'

He looked over, his expression somewhat incredulous. 'Are you still sulking about that?'

'I'm not sulking.'

'Absolutely you are.'

'Do you know what?' Ella muttered. 'Not everything goes back to you, Santo.'

'Of course it does.' It was the first smile she'd seen on him today, but it faded when he turned and saw her expression. 'That was a joke,' he said. 'So what's wrong?'

'It doesn't matter.'

'It does to me.'

Sometimes he could be so nice, just so damned nice, which was why he charmed so many, why he was so brilliant with women, Ella reminded herself.

'Are you having second thoughts about working for Luigi?' he asked as he added his signature to the paper she had brought for him to sign.

'No.' Which was an outright lie, since Ella had accepted the job she'd had five emails from her soon-to-be-boss, each one a touch more familiar. 'We need to sort out a time for your interviews with my replacement.'

'And when you no longer work for me, can we celebrate in bed?' He watched her eyes close for a second. 'Get used to it, Ella. If you think I'm a lech, you wait till you start your new job.'

'I never said you were a lech.'

'What then?'

'Let's just concentrate on work for now. Paulo can't come till next Sunday.'

'It will be the final day of filming.'

'If I can rearrange the ship.'

'You have to,' Santo said. 'We're getting nowhere.'

'Okay.' Ella sighed. 'I'm doing my best. I'll arrange for Paulo to come about four. You can do a brief interview in your trailer and then I'll take him out to dinner, while you lot all party.' She gave a tight smile, because the parties Santo threw at the end of filming were legendary, though the way this movie was going it might end up being more of a wake.

'What about the other one?'

'Marianna seems to think she should be discussing things directly with you.'

Santo merely shrugged. 'I'm a bit busy with other things to be sorting out interview times, Ella.'

'I know that. I was just letting you know. Okay, if there's nothing more you need me for here I'll head back to the hotel.'

'Stay,' Santo suggested. 'Rafaele is going to give the crying scene a rest, thank God, and work on the final kiss.'

That, she did not want to see, because she remembered them acting it out. But more than that, she wanted to give in to him, to just give in to herself and say yes.

'I have a ship to sort out.'

'Ella...' He could not stand this. He had never wanted someone so badly. He was turned on and pissed off and he did not understand why she was so reluctant to be with him, why she didn't even seem to want to talk to him.

Santo blew out a breath called frustration. He had been nothing but nice. The sex had been great and he had kept his distance. He didn't know what he was doing wrong. Finally there was a woman his user guide manual couldn't work out and he didn't like it a bit. 'I want to talk to you,' Santo said. 'Away from here. I am going to finish at seven tonight and then I am taking you out for dinner. No work—' he made it very clear '—there is no need to bring my diary. We are going out for dinner.'

'I don't think that's necessary.'

'It's very necessary…' he started, but he didn't get to finish because his assistant came to tell him that Taylor was getting upset.

'That's all I need.' Santo rolled his eyes and then turned to Ella. 'Can you talk to her, maybe have lunch with her. You're good with people. It might calm her down.'

'That's not my job, Santo.' And she should say nothing, Ella knew it, should just walk off and be done, except she couldn't resist. 'And I don't blame her for being upset—she's done an amazing job this morning. If Rafaele didn't get his shot, it has nothing to with Taylor. If I were directing we wouldn't be wasting so much time on the crying scene. I'd zoom into an Italian shot of Taylor crying, which could be done back in the studio if it doesn't work out here, and I wouldn't have Vince walking over to her. I'd have a moment of him watching and then Taylor turning, just his hand moving towards her face….' And she was sulking—oh, yes, she was—because it should be her directing this film, and with that she walked off.

And Santo stood there, when he wanted to chase after her.

Ella was affecting him in a way no woman ever had.

Since their time together she was all he had thought about—and for what?

He looked up and straight into the eyes of a pretty young actress who smiled straight back at him. If he just took her to his trailer he'd feel better in ten. He should just get over Ella in ways of old, but he was back to the wedding that never happened again—just utterly bored and unmoved by the usual temptations. He'd been working in the chocolate factory too long, perhaps, Santo realised, had possibly reached his fill, except he wasn't sure he wanted it over.

And for what?

For someone who didn't even want to talk to him?

For woman who was heading for Roma and that sleaze Luigi?

A moody, unreasonable, uptight woman who wasn't even a very good PA, Santo told himself.

So why had he hired her?

You know why, a small voice told him.

Because it wasn't for her PA skills that he wanted her around, and no, he hadn't been thinking with his head when, despite her terrible Italian, he'd kept her on.

And then he stopped thinking about Ella. Santo had no choice but to, as suddenly, albeit not completely un-expectedly, all hell broke loose on the set.

CHAPTER NINE

IT WASN'T ALL about Santo.

Ella had been telling the truth.

Today was the day she had been dreading for weeks now.

Calling home had always proven difficult, but in the past six months it had become almost impossible.

She put it off for as long as she could. Ella completed some of Santo's banking, rang and arranged the interview with Paulo and left a message for Marianna to call her. When she could put it off no longer, Ella dialled her parents' number and prayed that she'd get the answer machine.

She didn't.

'Hi, Mum.' Ella attempted upbeat. 'Happy birthday.'

'Ella!' She could hear the strain and discomfort in her mother's voice. No doubt she had been dreading this phone call too. There was just so little they had to say to each other. 'It's so lovely to hear from you— where are you?'

'We're on location, filming.' Ella did her best to be vague, but when her mother pressed for more information about her beloved homeland, Ella told her where she was.

'Oh!' There was silence for a moment. 'That is close to where I grew up.'

'I know.'

'Have you been to have a look at my village?'

'Not yet,' Ella said. 'I've been so busy with work and everything and the shooting is falling way behind.'

'Your aunts will be so excited to finally meet you,' Gabriella said. 'I told them so much about you, about your work in the film industry.'

'I'm not working in the film industry.' It was a very sore point. 'I'm a PA.'

'For now,' Gabriella said. 'But you don't need to tell your aunts that. You tell them how well you're doing, how good things are....' Ella could hear the veiled warning, the call to keep up the pretence, to carry on with the hopeless charade that everything was perfect. 'Or maybe it would be better for you to say nothing about work. I don't think it will be good if they know you are working for a Corretti.'

'I'm not going to lie.'

'I never ask you to lie. I just don't think they need to know everything. The Corretti name has a long history—it might not go down too well. You know how shocked I was when I found out who you were working for. That name is one that strikes fear into a lot of people and especially in my village.'

And finally, finally, there was something to talk about, a common ground they could share. Maybe her trip to Italy was worth it, because at last there was a mutual link. 'That family is dangerous,' her mother warned.

'I think things are very different now.'

'There are no changes. I saw on the news that the wedding between the Corretti and Battaglia families didn't go ahead.' Ella smiled, because since she had been a little girl her mother always had the Italian radio on. The one thing Ella had been able to do for her mother, to make her life a little more pleasurable, was to get satellite television so that she could watch the Italian news, which Gabriella did, all of the time. 'I remember only too well Salvatore's sons…'

'Carlo and Benito?'

'Morto!' her mum said. 'I still remember the night they died. My sister rang and I turned on the news.… Don't you remember?' And a memory unfurled then. Ella would have been about twenty. She could see her mother standing by the television screen, shouting, a huge warehouse fire being shown on the news. It had meant nothing to Ella at the time, but it meant so much more now. She listened more carefully than she had back then as her mother spoke of that night. 'It was no accident, whatever anyone says.'

'They were killed?' Ella felt a shiver run down her spine.

'Who knows?' Gabriella said. 'They have a lot of enemies. Some people said it could have been an insurance scam that went wrong. These are the people you are dealing with—you should remember that at all times.'

'Santo is nothing like that,' Ella said.

'Please,' her mother scoffed. 'He is Carlo's son. He could be no other way. Carlo was obsessed with power, with money, with women—he could not stay faithful to his wife for even five minutes. Oh, but he was a charmer too.' Maybe Santo did take after his father after all. 'Salvatore was the worst.'

'Did he cheat too?'

'Who knows?' Gabriella said again. 'He was just pure bad—the Battaglia family too. How they ever slept at night with their consciences...' Gabriella said. 'Their wives were as bad too. Lording over everyone as if they were royalty, holding their fancy dinner parties. Your aunt worked in the kitchen of Salvatore's wife, Teresa, once for a dinner party. Their money was filthy—you ask your aunts. They will tell you—oh, the stories you will hear....' Then her voice cracked as a huge pang of homesickness hit. Gabriella missed her sisters so very much, but it wasn't just them. She missed her home, her village and her history too. 'I wish I could speak with them. I mean, I know we speak on the phone but I want to see them. I wish I could be there when you all meet. I want to show you my village....'

'Mum...' Ella's voice was thick with unshed tears. 'Why don't you come over?'

'Please, Ella, you know it is not possible.'

'Just for a holiday. I will pay your airfare...' But Ella stopped then. She was just repeating herself and, given it was her mother's birthday, Ella didn't pursue it further. She didn't want to upset her today. 'I'll go and visit everyone soon and give them all your love.'

'Let me know when you go, so I can ring them and tell them to expect you.'

'Okay.' Ella could not manage upbeat even a single second longer. 'I really do have to get to work now. I love you, Mum.'

'I love you too, Ella. Do you want to speak with your—'

It was Ella who hung up.

She was actually shaking with anger as she did so. That her mother could even suggest that she speak with her father after all that had gone on, that still she was supposed to pretend that terrible day had never happened.

Yet it had.

She could not break down again, but she could no longer pretend to forget either. She looked into the mirror, lifted her hair and saw the pink scar. The scar was proof that that day had happened. It was even there when she smiled. Those lovely white teeth had come at the most terrible price. Ella could still remember spitting her own teeth into her hand, but worse than that was the memory of the betrayal—that her mother could have forgiven him and stayed.

That she could watch as her own daughter was beaten and, instead of calling the police, had stood there sobbing and screaming. Instead of calling for an ambulance, she had handed Ella ice packs and told the story to give to the dentist, to the doctor. Had told Ella that if she didn't want to make it worse for her mother, then she must tell everyone that she fell.

Ella needed to get out, to walk, to run. It was the reason she opened her door, for she would never have opened the door to Santo in this state. She wasn't crying, but she was still shaking in anger, still holding in a scream that wanted to come out.

'Ella?'

She brushed past him, but he caught her wrist.

'Please, Santo.' She was having great trouble keeping her voice from shouting. 'I was just about to go for a walk.'

'Later...' He simply could not let her walk off like this. He could see how upset she was.

'I just need to get out for a while.'

'Of course you do.' Santo was very practical. 'We all go a bit stir-crazy in the hotel after a few days. I'll take you for a drive. I could use one too.' He was not going to argue about this. He had come to visit Ella for rather more pressing reasons than a drive, but for once, work could wait.

They drove, in silence at first, around the winding streets, but Santo drove the powerful car with far more finesse than Ella and it was actually nice to sit back and stare at the scenery.

'It's beautiful.' Ella looked at the dotted beige buildings built into the hills and then they turned into a village. Another one, Santo explained, that was run-down and in much need of the new lease of life the redevelopment might bring.

'There is only one café now,' he explained, slowing the car down. Ella peered up a long set of steps. 'Do you want to stop for a drink?'

Ella shook her head.

'There are only a couple of shops....' She was starting to understand more and more the difference this movie could make. It was such a stunning part of the country. There were just picture-perfect views everywhere. Yet so many, like her mother, had left. She blinked and turned her head as she passed vaguely familiar buildings, recognising some of them from the photos her mother spent a long time reminiscing over.

'This is my mother's village.'

'I know.' Santo turned and smiled. 'You could drop in on your aunts now.'

'I don't think so.' Ella gave a tight smile.

'Probably a good call,' Santo said. 'Your mother would never hear the last of it if you arrived with a Corretti in tow.'

'Slow down a moment.' He did so. 'I think that's the baker's that my mother used to work at before she moved.'

'Does she work now?'

'No,' Ella said. 'She worked in a factory till she had me, then gave it up to help out in my father's shop.' She peered into the window as Santo slowly passed. 'It's nice to see it.' It really was. There were a few people walking, and some women sitting in the front of their gardens talking. And it was actually nice to see it for the first time with Santo rather than alone. She took a breath. 'Could we get that coffee?'

'Sure.' He turned the car around on a very narrow road with a very steep descent on one side. Only that wasn't what had the sweat beading on Ella's forehead. She should take a moment to touch up her make-up. She was supposed to look nice at all times, but she wasn't actually working, Ella realised.

This was very personal indeed.

They walked along the narrow pavement. Even the street was cobbled—it was like stepping back in history. They stopped outside a tiny church.

'My mum gets so upset when anyone gets married.

She's told me all about the church. She says the parties afterwards are amazing....'

'The whole street comes out,' Santo said. 'Tables are set up for the reception.'

'It's just so different from anything I'm used to,' Ella said. 'Not just here, the whole of Italy. Everything's so much newer in Australia, even the old buildings aren't comparatively old.' She looked around at the relatively unchanged architecture, could completely understand how her mother missed it, how Gabriella could still picture it so well, because it was just as it appeared in the photos. 'Nothing's changed,' Ella said.

'Of course it has,' Santo responded. 'The changes just don't show.'

They climbed the narrow steps to a café and certainly they turned heads when they walked in. Ella was quite sure it was because Santo was a Corretti, and that it had nothing to do with the fact he was possibly the most beautiful man in the world.

The whole place fell silent and they were shepherded to a seat.

'Are they scared of you?' Ella asked in a low voice. 'Or angry?'

'Both,' Santo said. 'I hope soon they will be neither.'

He ordered—coffee and crêpes that were filled with gelato. It was just so nice to be away from set. The locals were starting to talk amongst themselves again, and yes, the gelato was as good as her mother described.

'It's nice to be out, thanks for this.'

'No problem.'

'How come you're not on set?'

He just shrugged—those reasons could wait. For

now Santo just wanted to talk about her. 'Your mother's never been back?'

'Nope.'

'One day, maybe?'

Ella didn't answer.

Even when they were back in the car, when he tried to work out just what it was that had upset her so much today, still Ella spoke about work.

'I spoke with Paulo and arranged his interview and I left a message for Marianna. Paulo sounds really good, he's just not able to start yet.'

'Which is a problem,' Santo admitted. 'I need someone who can start as soon as possible.' He had, Ella realised, stopped trying to dissuade her from leaving. 'What about Marianna?'

'The truth?' Ella checked. It was nice to be chatting, nice to be driving and away from everything, and just so very nice to be with Santo.

'The truth,' Santo confirmed.

'She's awful,' Ella said. 'She's incredibly confident, treated me like I was her secretary, wanted to only deal directly with you. She refused to give an inch when I tried to pin her for a time to come in for an interview.' Ella rolled her eyes. 'To sum up, I think she'll be perfect for the job.'

'I thought I already had perfect.'

He glanced over and reluctantly she smiled. 'No, we both know that you didn't.' Maybe it was because Santo was so open and honest, that in this, Ella found that she was able to be. 'I'm not tough enough.'

'I don't always like tough.'

'I'm not...' She didn't really know how to say it,

how to admit just how much it all had hurt her. 'I don't think Marianna will sulk if you don't send her flowers.'

'So you were sulking.'

'Yes.'

'What else is Marianna good at?'

'Multi-tasking apparently.' She looked out of the window at the ocean and the beauty of the day and hated her melancholy, hated that she hadn't been able to play by the rules and happily tumble in bed with him without adding her heart to the equation. 'She'd probably be taking dictation now and giving you a quick hand-job as she did so.' Ella turned to the sound of his laughter, realised she was smiling now too, because that was how he made her feel. Yes, it was so good to get out.

He pulled the car over and he just smiled as she sat there blushing, as the best lover in the world, as the man she had so foolishly thought she could bear to lose, cupped her face.

'I walked into a storm that morning—I lost my director, I had stuff going on with my family, I had my brother out at sea.'

'I know, I know.'

'But when I knew you were arriving I did arrange flowers,' Santo said. 'I had them sent to the room, the same room that you took one look at and left. And I organised dinner—I really wanted to tell you how much our time together had meant, how I was looking forward to seeing you, how it killed not ring—' He looked at her for the longest time. 'Who hurt you?' He saw her rapid blink. 'Is there an ex-husband?' He saw her frown.

'Of course not.'

'What do you mean "of course"?' Santo said. 'I know

nothing about you, Ella. What I do know I could write on a Post-it note. I know your parents are together, that there are no brothers or sisters, that your mother is from here.' He saw the well of tears in the bottom of her eyes. 'That the sex was like nothing I have ever known, but I don't know you....'

'You're my boss, you don't need—'

'I'm your lover!' He almost shouted it. 'Get it into your head.'

'For how long though...' She hated the neediness, but it was the truth, because he was telling her to open up to him, to give him more than sex, and she was terrified to.

'Who knows?' He was completely honest. 'But if we can't talk, then not for much longer.'

'You don't talk about the stuff that troubles you.'

'I've tried more than you,' Santo said.

'Santo, I don't tell anyone...' She was close to panic now. 'I don't share myself with anyone and I'm not going to start pouring my heart out to you.'

'You will.' The view was more stunning than the ocean behind him——his eyes so intense, the passion blazing——and she was there in his spotlight now. He would strip her bare and she was petrified, not just of it ending, but of the togetherness too. She could simply not envisage sharing herself so completely with another, of trusting another. 'Tell and kiss.' She could feel the warmth of his skin so close and she teased his translation, just as he did to her.

'It's kiss and tell.'

'No.' His eyes were open. Santo had made up his mind and he moved back and started the engine. 'It's tell and kiss.' And as he drove off, as always he made her smile. He took her hand and placed it in his lap. 'Though, of course, I don't mind a woman who can multi-task.'

'Ha, ha…' She took back her hand.

They had been out for a couple of hours and he knew no more than he had when she had opened her hotel door.

'What was it like?' He turned to her question. 'I mean, back there, in the café. People were nervous just to see you.…'

'That is because I would rarely go there, but here…' He nodded ahead. 'They are more used to us. This is where my nonna lives.'

'But what was it like?'

It was Santo who couldn't answer. He could see his grandparents' house, huge and imposing and the keeper of so many secrets.

'Have you seen today's papers?' He didn't wait for her response, he knew that she had. 'There is far more to come. Always it is about power—that is how it is, that is how you are taught—but sometimes you just want to walk in a café and have coffee.' Ella nodded. 'That is why I like being on set—I am just Santo there. Of course, there are a few awkward looks today, given what has been said in the newspapers about my mother. I just have to wear it. Battaglia is determined to crush us and will stop at nothing—so now he makes sure that every piece of filth he can find ends up in the papers.' He looked at Ella. 'There is a lot of filth.'

There was, Santo knew that, but there was a lot of good too, and somehow he wanted to show her that. But there was something he, too, had been putting off for a while, something that might be easier with Ella by his side.

'Now,' Santo said, 'I take you where I have taken no woman before.' He glanced over to see her wide-eyed reaction. 'My nonna's.'

'Do you think that's a good idea?'

'Probably not.' Santo shrugged. 'She will have us married off in her mind the moment we walk in there, but I really ought to visit her. She will be very upset with all that is going on in the family and she is worried about Alessandro too, as well as mourning her husband. She never really got over losing her sons....' He was pensive for a moment. 'You know, for all that the cousins do not get on, for all the arguments, the one thing that unites us is our love for her—she is a good woman.' Perhaps Ella's silence spoke volumes, for Santo turned his head in instant defence. 'She is.'

'Of course,' came Ella guarded response. Salvatore Corretti's reputation was legendary, and if Ella knew a little of what had gone on to get there, then absolutely his wife must have known a whole lot more.

'Her family hated that she married him,' Santo explained a little, 'but she loved him, and turned a blind eye to all that he got up to.'

Ella bit down on her lip in an effort not to voice her thoughts.

'Sometimes it is easier to, perhaps...' Santo said.

'Or simply more convenient.' Ella could not stay silent on this. 'I'm sorry, Santo. I'm trying not to judge your nonna—I haven't met her after all—but I don't buy that turn a blind eye excuse.'

'And I am not asking you to.' He saw her tense profile. 'I'm just letting you know, before we go in there, that these past years have been very hard on her. These are exceptionally difficult times, so just…' He shook his head. 'It doesn't matter.'

As they approached Ella was both nervous and excited to be meeting such a legend. It was like being invited backstage and the chance to meet the matriarch of this family was just too good to pass up. But as they walked towards the house she could see Santo's strained face.

'I'm not going to say anything that might offend her.'

'I know you wouldn't,' Santo said, or he would never have brought here.

CHAPTER TEN

A MAID LET them in, but rather than standing and waiting in the hall, Santo took Ella's hand and they walked straight through, Santo calling out to announce he was here.

'Santo!' There was a crow of surprise as Teresa heard them and they were in the large lounge before she was even standing. There was a flurry of kisses and introductions. Teresa was dressed from head to toe in black, and from the candle burning by a bible on a table, it was clear she was deep in mourning. But there was absolute pleasure on the old woman's face as she greeted her grandson. There was no denying the bond was a genuine one and that Teresa was so pleased to see him.

'It is lovely to meet you,' Teresa said to Ella. 'Such a nice surprise—you will forgive me if my English is not very good.' She smiled. 'And you are to correct me if I forget and speak in Italian,' she added to Santo. 'My mind is everywhere at the moment.'

'Don't worry,' Santo said. 'Anyway, Ella's mother is from here, so she speaks a little Italian.' He smiled and so, too, did Ella.

'He is teasing you, yes?' Teresa checked and then answered her own question. 'Of course he is.'

Santo brought such a smile to her weary face. He was incredibly good with women—all women—because he didn't mind a bit when she cried a little when they spoke of Salvatore. 'The house, it is too quiet,' she said, 'but then I tell myself at least he is not dealing with all this, at least he died thinking that the families would unite.'

'It will sort,' Santo said, but Teresa shook her head.

'I am not so sure that it will. Have you heard from Alessandro?'

'He is okay.' Santo was so gentle with her. 'I saw him the morning after and he has texted me a couple of times. He just needs time.'

'And the rest of the family? Have you seen Luca?'

'I am staying out of it as much as I can for now.' Santo was firm. He certainly didn't want to discuss the scandals that were going on with his nonna. 'The better we do with this film, the better it will be for the family, for everyone. The locals are watching the filming. The docklands are busy, for the first time in a long time. This is what I need to give my attention to now.'

'But even that is having problems!' Teresa kept her eyes on everything, Ella realised. 'That actress...' Teresa screwed up her nose. 'I saw the photos—she should be ashamed.'

'It does take two.' Santo grinned.

'So, how is she doing?' Teresa asked and the smile wavered on Santo's face.

'Taylor's a very good actress,' Ella spoke then. 'Well, she's got a lot of potential, if she had the right person directing to bring it out.'

'Ella thinks she should be directing.' Santo's voice was wry, but he was glad for the change in conversation, because it was clear Teresa was getting more and more upset. The challenges the family faced were not going to be easily fixed and he hated that she was sitting alone and fretting.

'You have a problem with a female director?' Teresa teased.

'Oh, I have no issues with Ella being a woman.' Santo grinned but then his phone went. 'Excuse me, I have to take this.'

As he went outside to take the call, Teresa poured them two small glasses of limoncello. It was tart and lovely and tasted just like her mother made and she told Teresa the same.

'There are many recipes, but this is the local one. Your mother would make it the same way. Have you been to visit where she lived yet?'

'Santo took me there on the way here,' Ella said. 'I am going to visit my aunts when we finish shooting.'

'And your mother, does she love Australia? I have heard so many good things about it.'

And Ella sat quiet for a moment, sipped on her limoncello and answered carefully. 'It's a beautiful country,' Ella said, 'but my mother misses home an awful lot.'

'Of course,' Teresa said. 'But she is happy with her choice?'

And she looked at Ella for a very long time. There was a moment, a long one, and one Ella decided where it would be prudent to play by very old rules. It was, Ella told herself, a practice run for her aunties. 'Very happy,' Ella said and returned Teresa's smile, looking up in relief when Santo came in.

'Take Ella and show her the winery,' Teresa said. 'Choose something nice for dinner tonight.'

'You have to get back, don't you?' Santo said to Ella. It was nice that he offered the choice as to whether they stay longer, but Ella knew it would be rude to leave now, knew from her mother what was silently expected.

'No.' Ella smiled. 'I've got everything done. Dinner would be lovely.'

'She seems to like you.' They were walking in the grounds, through the vines and out to the winery. She'd have loved to take a photo, to tell her mum she was here, but she wasn't sure that that suggestion would be particularly welcomed.

'You're quiet,' she commented, because Santo rarely was.

'It feels different to be here and know he isn't.'

'Sorry...' Ella could have kicked herself for her own insensitivity. 'I didn't think.'

'No!' Santo shook his head. 'I am not upset.'

'I do understand that whatever has gone on, still he was your grandparent.'

'It's not fond memories I'm having, Ella.' Santo said no more than that. They walked into the cool dark winery and she wondered if here he might try something, but instead Santo spent an awful long time choosing the wine.

'This one,' he said. 'This was from the year you were born.'

'I didn't know you knew the year I was born.'

'I read your résumé.' He gave her a smile and walked over, lifted his hand to her hair, just wondered about her, really. 'You know I always wanted to have sex in here.'

He was just so direct.

'With your grandmother waiting in the house?'

'That doesn't come into my fantasy.'

'Well, it's a bit off-putting in mine,' Ella said. She was terribly wary of him, trying to keep things light when she felt anything but, trying to keep her head on during a most difficult of days.

'I miss you.' He watched her frown.

'You don't know me.'

'That's what I miss.'

He didn't even try to kiss her, did nothing other than take her hand and walk back to the house. She just couldn't read his mood.

The food was heavenly—fennel salad dripping in the best olive oil Ella had tasted, and a huge lasagne, but the Sicilian way, stuffed with Italian sausage and cheeses.

Santo sat at the table, chatted and spoke and smiled in all the right places, and she tried to fathom him, but couldn't. He looked up and caught her staring, and smiled till she blushed as he stared back and he pressed his foot to her leg just once, but it wasn't Santo.

It was like watching an actor play his part.

'Do you remember my birthday?' Teresa smiled and recounted tales of supposed happier times, but Ella watched a muscle flicker in Santo's cheek as Teresa mentioned Benito's children and asked after Luca and Gio, though she was wise enough perhaps to not mention Matteo. 'And that time Lia hid and we could not find her for hours. You were so young then. Grace was still alive.'

'Grace?'

'Lia's mum,' Santo explained. 'Benito was married

before Simona.' He was so much more open here, but then so was Teresa, Ella realised. She must assume, given that Santo had brought her here, that they were serious.

'She lived with us,' Teresa explained. 'When Grace died.' And she smiled over to Santo, and Ella watched as there was just a brief pause before Santo duly smiled back, not that Teresa noticed. She turned her attention to Ella.

'Will you tell your mother that you ate with me?' Her eyes twinkled.

'I can't wait to tell her.' Ella laughed, because she'd been sitting there thinking just that. For the first time in a very long time, she actually missed her mother, wished that today was something they could have properly shared.

'She will be shocked, and she will warn you about me, but also she will love to know!' Teresa promised, and it was as if she had met her mother—she just knew what she was like. 'She will want every single detail,' Teresa said as the maid brought in a huge tray of sweet canelloni, 'but even as you give her the details she will tell you that you should not have come!'

'Then she'll ask me to tell her about your furniture.'

He watched as the two women sat laughing, and thank God he'd brought Ella with him, because Santo wasn't sure he could have got through this visit alone, and certainly not as well. Memories were churning. The happy birthdays his nonna all too frequently regaled were not quite as perfect, if Santo remembered correctly.

And he was quite sure he did.

Surprisingly it was Santo who declined coffee.

He just wanted out.

Even as they left, Teresa was plying her with bottles of olive oil and limoncello and, even as they climbed in the car, offering them to come back in for coffee.

'We really have to go,' Santo said. 'We need to get back to the Olympic Village.'

Thankfully his little dig went straight over Teresa's head.

'That wasn't funny,' Ella said, her cheeks scalding as he started up the car.

'I thought it was.' Santo smirked. 'You know, I think sex actually enhances performance.'

'I'll draft a letter to the IOC for you,' Ella said tartly. 'I'm sure they'll welcome your thoughts.'

'Do you?' She turned and saw that his expression was serious. 'Can you talk to me? Can you tell me why you were so upset when I came to your room this afternoon?'

And he'd shared so much with her today that maybe she could. There was this argument raging but it was dimming. Quite simply, with Santo she wanted to share—she just didn't know how. 'It's my mum's birthday today,' Ella admitted. 'I'd just called her when you came to my room.' Santo said nothing. 'I find it really hard to talk to her.'

'You don't get on?'

'I don't agree with some of her choices,' Ella said and then amended, 'I don't agree with a lot of her choices.'

She said nothing more for a while, and neither did Santo. He was waiting for her to talk to him and she tried to a couple of times, opened her mouth to speak, then closed it again. It was twenty-seven years of silence that she was fighting to break and it was especially difficult to break that silence to a man.

Except Santo was like no man she had ever met and maybe she was starting to actually trust him, maybe it was time that she opened up. As they drove in to the hotel and the valet approached, just as he went to open her door, Ella spoke.

'My father is an alcoholic.'

As she went to climb out of the car he caught her wrist and gently pulled her back. 'For that you get a kiss.'

He ignored the open doors, the people standing in the foyer, the valet waiting to take his keys. Instead, as promised, he gave her a kiss for telling, and she was crying as he did so, because she'd never actually said those words before. Then his tongue was on her cheeks, taking her tears. It was a very private, very thorough kiss, in a very public place, but right now, neither cared a fraction.

'Let's get inside,' Santo said.

Once they were out, he took her hand and they walked towards the hotel. Clearly he had to let it go, ought to let go, for they were about to step into the revolving door, but it was as if they were glued together, as if neither could bear to be apart, not even for a second, and they walked into the door together.

'He beats her.' She just said it out loud in a tiny space and, oblivious of onlookers, not caring that no one could now get in or out of the hotel, as promised, he rewarded her with his mouth, just pulled her right into him. They were the only two people left in the world.

He could have taken her there had he wanted to. There was just this slow unfurling of her heart as he held and kissed her, and in that moment, Ella truly thought she could tell him anything. For the first time in her life, she trusted another with her heart.

'Now,' Santo said, 'I take you to bed and then after—' because there would be after '—if you want to, we can talk some more.'

Ella, weak from admission, was grateful for the chance of a reprieve from her confessions. As he pushed the glass door, as they walked through the entrance, all she wanted was his bed, his warmth, the shield of him that for far too long she had denied.

'Santo Corretti...'

It felt as if she were being rapidly brought out of an anaesthetic, the antidote to surrender shooting through her veins, as a stunning woman walked towards them and the safe, warm feeling she had, so briefly, sampled was suddenly threatened. The bubble of bliss burst, and his arm, around her, squeezed suddenly tense shoulders.

'I am Marianna...' She smiled warmly to Santo, but it turned black when she greeted Ella. 'Your replacement.'

'Now is not a good time.' Santo was extremely curt. 'I do not do impromptu interviews. You can arrange a time with Ella for tomorrow.'

'No...' Ella just wanted it over and done with. She could hardly blame Marianna for jumping on a plane to convince the boss personally—hadn't Ella done exactly the same? 'You two go ahead, I need to...' She didn't even try to come up with an excuse. 'Tomorrow you are busy with filming. It might be better if we can sort this all out tonight.'

Ella ignored Santo as he tried to call her back. Instead she pulled back the gate to the lift and headed to her room, horribly unsettled at the turn of events, but possibly glad for them.

She had been so close to telling everything, to opening up and pouring out her heart.

But for what?

She was leaving, moving to Rome in a few short weeks—what hope was there for them anyway? Santo couldn't even manage longevity in a normal relationship, a long-distance one was surely an impossible ask.

Ella needed to think. She had sworn to never cry over him, to not give this playboy her heart, and she had just come dangerously close to doing so. She opened the door to her room and there was a huge bunch of flowers waiting there. They brought a very watery smile to her lips. Santo had been on and off the phone for a lot of the afternoon, and though she was touched at his thoughtfulness, as she opened the attached card, Ella braced herself for more of his endearments, reminded herself that Santo was a stunning flirter, yet she found herself frowning as she read the card.

You will be amazing.
See why I had to sleep with you before I told you?
Santo xxx
P.S. You're fired.

She didn't understand his cryptic message, but knew this evening she had been played, that, all day, sex had

been on his agenda, that it had been an absolute certainty for Santo that the day would end in his bed.

And, had it not been for Marianna, it would have.

She poured herself some limoncello from the bottle
Teresa had given her, tried to tell herself that she must
calm down, tried to work out what his message meant.
Not liking where her thoughts were leading, that once in
bed he'd take away the problem of her working for him,
no doubt, right now, he was giving Marianna the job.

How bloody convenient for him.

'Ella...' She had known that he would come to her
room, that Santo would have to offer a rapid explanation for his message, and she was very tight-lipped as
she opened the door. 'You got the flowers....' There
was an attempt at a joke, when Ella really wasn't in the
mood for one. 'Now do you see why I need a PA? Even
flowers I manage to screw up.'

'So you were going to fire me, after you slept with
me.'

'No, no, you have it all wrong.'

'I was a dead certainty, was I?'

'Yes.' He made no apology about it. 'I was certain
that tonight I was going to make love to you.'

'So, how was Marianna?'

'She was everything that you said she was. Ella,
please, will you just listen?'

'You don't want me to hang around and train her up?'

'Ella...'

She didn't let him get a word in.

'Because it shouldn't take long—I've streamlined
the process....'

'Really!' Santo's raised an eyebrow. He actually rather liked her angry. 'How so?'

'Well, you're a full-time job, but not a very complicated one. She watched his tongue roll in his cheek. 'I'll just hand her the Santo Bag.'

'The Santo Bag?'

'It contains all the essentials.'

And she took the huge bag she'd been carrying around and adding to for four months now, and tipped the contents onto his bed.

'New white shirt, grey tie, black tie…' She glanced over and there was a very unrepentant smile curving on his lips. 'You do seem to attend an inordinate amount of funerals.'

'The company I keep,' Santo said, because actors lived and played hard as well, 'and I have a complicated family too.'

'Headache pills,' Ella said. 'And sunglasses.'

Santo said nothing.

'Condoms—you tend to run out an awful lot.' Tears pricked at her eyes as she remembered a frantic 3:00 a.m. phone call from her boss, and she was so blisteringly angry with him, so completely furious with herself for loving him. Loathing him too, for all he had, however unwittingly, put her heart through, because it had killed to see him with others.

'We shoot in strange locations.' But he wasn't smiling now, realising now the depth of her hurt, because until last week there hadn't been any hint that she even liked him.

'First aid kit and those amazing gel Band-Aids…'

She heard his breathing come angry and hard as she reminded him of one time. 'Great for carpet burn.'

'I get the message, Ella.'

'Oh, I haven't finished yet. Antiseptic…' she continued. 'Great for scratches.'

'You were jealous.' He was angry with himself for not seeing it, angry with her too, for all she had put herself through. 'All that time…'

'Jealous!' She snorted. 'I'm not jealous, Santo, I'm sick of it. You don't need a PA following you around—you need a school nurse!'

And she hated him for smiling then, hated the stealth of his approach. Yes, she was jealous, had, even though she'd denied it, been hot, spitting jealous and even worse than that, now he knew.

'Do you know what you need?'

He picked a condom up from the bed and then he tossed it. 'Oh, that's right, we don't use them.'

'Of all the arrogant—' He hushed her with his mouth, pushed her against the wall with a kiss so violent there was a clash of enamel and she tried to push him off.

'You do need it,' Santo said, refusing to release her, his hands pushing up her skirt. 'You need a quick reminder of how good we are. And then we're going to talk.'

'When you fire me?' she spat out.

'When I hire you.' He reclaimed her mouth as he tore at her panties and—love him or loathe him, she didn't know—all Ella knew was that she was kissing him back. She'd never had angry sex before, had never been caught in a row that came with pure passion. At the return of her kiss he lifted her and she found that he was backing her into another wall, his mouth still on hers as he spoke. 'I was going to offer you a job....'

'As what? Your on-set tart?'

Right now she'd take it. She was kissing him back and grappling with his zipper. 'I hate you, Santo,' she told him. 'I hate that you planned this.'

'You love it.'

He lifted her onto him, and she hated more the legs that so willingly wrapped around him, but then, he'd taken off that shackle. This was no threat to her job. As of now, she didn't work for him, and she found herself feeling surprisingly free.

'You love it, more than you want to admit to it.' He was inside her and she was grinding down. 'You are the most uptight woman I know,' Santo said, 'except in the bedroom.' She was starting to come and trying to hold on to it. 'Guess what?' He was battering into her, not just her sex but her head. 'I accept that...' He went to say something more, but gave in. She could hear the neighbours banging on the wall as Santo switched to rapid Italian, heard her own moans and shouts as they locked into oblivion. He was right, she loved it. She was just petrified of loving him.

'I have to change rooms.' She was leaning on him, stunned and a bit dizzy, never wanting to face her neighbours again, but Santo lifted her chin to face him.

'There's something I came to tell you this afternoon.' Ella looked up at him. 'I fired Rafaele.'

He was an absolute gentleman. He took her shredded panties and put them in the bin, retrieved a wayward shoe and even smoothed her skirt for her as she processed the news. It was huge to fire a director mid-shoot and she didn't dare hope, didn't dare dream. He tucked in his shirt and did everything up, a strange attempt to separate this from the bedroom, except she could feel him trickling between her thighs.

'Ella, I have given a lot of thought as to his replacement and I think you would make an amazing director.'

'Santo.' She ran a tongue over her lip, a lip swollen from passion and the bruising crush of his kiss. 'I don't know what to say. Is it because you can't get anyone else?'

'I have three people who can fly out tonight.' He scuppered that argument with a flick of his wrist.

'Then is it because…' She couldn't even bring herself to say it. 'Santo, you're right. I should never have considered you doing me a favour just because we slept with each other.'

'It has nothing to do with sex.' He was almost stern as he said it. 'I would never hire for that reason, never. A director's role is too important. I am only hiring you because I now think you are right for the role. I have given it some serious thought and have come to the conclusion that you would be fantastic—you understand the movie inside out. You have seen the disaster Rafaele has made…'

Ella nodded.

'And you know what the movie needs.'

'Taylor would never agree.'

'She already has,' Santo said. 'There was a lot of trouble on set today. Things turned very nasty and, you're right, it is not her acting that is at fault. I spoke to her at length. That is when I told her your suggestions and how passionate you are about this film. She is happy to work with you.'

'Really?'

'Fresh vision is always good,' Santo said. 'So here is your chance.'

She was terrified, because his earlier argument had been right. She hadn't earned her stripes. She hadn't even been an assistant. If she took this role Ella would be stepping straight into the big league and she told him that.

'You can do it,' Santo said. 'I have every faith that you can handle this, but it's the last professional hand-hold I will give you, Ella. We will be fighting tomorrow on set. I am not going to hold back just because it is you—and if I don't think you are doing well...' Then he paused. She didn't need to be told. Ella knew only too well how he operated. 'But when we are off set...' He waited and he watched as she shook her head. 'Ella, I promise you that whatever happens between us on a personal level I will not bring it to work.'

'I can't.' She couldn't, but she knew more explanation was needed. Santo had offered her the biggest break professionally, and also emotionally. She had never opened up more with another, and she needed to do so now. 'I only slept with you when I knew I had the other job.'

'I know,' Santo said. He had no issues with truths. 'You left your email open on my computer.'

'My mum used to work for my father.'

'You are not your mother.'

'I know that,' Ella said.

'And this is very different...'

'I know, but I swore a long time ago that my career would always come first, that I would never jeopardise it for a man, any man. I've broken way too many of my own rules lately but this really is a big chance. It's not a PA job that I don't particularly want that I'm risking now. I can't go back on my promise to myself just because it's you.'

And she waited for his argument, for him to attempt to dissuade, but it never came. 'I accept that.' And only now did she understand the true meaning of his earlier words, that he had known from the start what her rules would be.

'It's a couple of weeks,' Ella said. 'I need to concentrate properly on the film.'

'Then do,' Santo said. 'But understand this, Ella—you don't get to pick and choose.'

'Sorry?'

'Till filming is over you are in or out.'

Ella just looked at him, wasn't entirely sure she understood what he was saying.

'You don't get to dip in when you choose to,' Santo clarified. 'So what is it to be—in or out.'

And for Ella, there could only be one answer. 'Out.'

'Fine.' He headed for the door. 'Good luck. As my note said—you'll be amazing.'

CHAPTER ELEVEN

SANTO BLINKED IN surprise when he walked on the set this morning, not because Ella was there. He'd known she'd be early. More it was an Ella he had never seen.

She was wearing a faded denim skirt and espadrilles and a halter neck top. The hair that was usually groomed was hanging loose as it did in the bedroom. As she smiled at him, Santo saw she was wearing absolutely no make-up.

'Is this director Ella?' he asked as she walked over to him.

'No, this is Ella.'

And it was a bit of a fist to the gut, that all the clothes and the make-up had been the part she had played for him, and just confirmed that Santo didn't know her at all.

'The ship is all organised.' Marianna came over and spoke in Italian with Santo as Ella half listened, translating easily. Yes, Marianna was a far more efficient PA. She had achieved in a few hours what Ella had been struggling with for days. 'So everyone will be in place for 5:00 a.m. and it sails at 3:00 p.m. the following day.'

'Eccellente.' He glanced over to Ella. 'We have to be finished by then.'

'We will be.'

Santo nodded and turned back to Marianna, telling her to organise a party that final night for the crew. That was the one part of the job Ella had loved doing. Santo knew how to throw a good party and Ella had enjoyed organising them. She mentioned a couple of contacts she had to Marianna.

'I can run through things this evening,' Ella offered. 'I'm sorry, I really haven't been much help handing over.'

'No need,' Marianna said. 'I have my own contacts. Anyway, I'll speak with Santo if I need to know anything. I prefer to find out things firsthand.' She went to head off and then changed her mind. 'Actually, I need his spare car keys, his diary, that sort of thing....'

Ella was terribly aware of Santo's smirk as she went in her bag and handed over a few items.

'You forgot the sunglasses,' Santo said.

'So I did,' Ella responded tartly, her cheeks burning as she handed them over.

'Headache tablets,' he prompted.

'No need,' Marianna chimed in. 'I have some on me.'

Ella's bag was soon considerably emptier as she handed over a shirt and a couple of ties too.

'I think that's everything,' Ella said.

'Sure?' Santo checked, enjoying her discomfort.

'I'm sure Marianna is prepared for every eventuality.' Ella smiled sweetly and then turned her attention back to what was important, what would remain.

Work.

Except she wanted to share it with him.

To start with, Ella was incredibly nervous. It seemed

wrong to be giving directions to someone as skilled as Taylor, but overriding her nerves was the rising thrill that Taylor seemed to completely understand her.

'You're not happy as such,' Ella said, trying not to be too rude about Rafaele's interpretation. 'It's more that you're carefree. Yes, you know he's leaving tomorrow, but for now you have no idea what's to come.' She looked through the viewfinder, watched Taylor walking along the beach with her lover who would soon go missing, watched the shot of her life before it changed for ever, and any nerves Ella had died then, because she could do this.

All those endless nights of her childhood spent locked in her room making movies with her mind reaped the rewards today as finally a scene came to life, and there were actually tears in her eyes as Ella watched it unfold.

And Santo watched her grow before his eyes too.

'Vince, from now on you're not going to be watching her.' Ella got back to the heart of the script. Rafaele had interpreted it that Vince came upon Taylor crying, but over and over Ella had read it and pictured it differently. Now she brought it to life. 'You need to be here first, thinking about your friend, then you see Taylor arrive. Remember that till this point you've never really liked her. You've always thought that she was using him, but watching her cry, you see for the first time how much she loves him—it is that that moves you.'

'Right.' The sulking Vince actually smiled because, till now, Rafaele had made his character look nothing other than a man taking advantage of a vulnerable woman.

'That's why you go over,' Ella said to Vince. 'You realise that she knows how you feel, that you both miss him. And, Taylor…' Ella said. 'When he turns around, you're defensive. You're used to him making sarcastic comments. He's already accused you of crocodile tears, but it is his empathy that is going to have you two heading off to the beach.'

'Got it.'

'And we're not going to do the full-on crying scene yet…' Santo watched as Taylor breathed out in relief. The past few days had been draining at best. 'Just a few tears. What I want to get is your expression when Vince joins you.'

Taylor was brilliant. For the first time since filming had started Santo could breathe. Just having Vince there first changed everything, shifted the whole dynamics. It was something he wouldn't have thought of and he told Ella the same as they headed back to the hotel.

'We've got more done today than we have all week.'

She was glowing inside at the praise, on a high from finally doing the job she loved and knowing that she was doing it well.

'I'm starving,' Santo said. It was 10:00 p.m. and they had been too busy working to stop and take advantage of the catering. Now, all Ella wanted to do was to order something from room service, or… She looked over to Santo as they walked through the foyer. Perhaps they could have dinner and talk about the scenes tomorrow, or perhaps—Ella took a deep breath—they could simply talk.

'So am I.' She was beyond conflicted, wavering as to the choice she had earlier made. Santo would do noth-

ing to jeopardise this film over something that might
happen between them. And he was right—she was not
her mother. She was so much stronger than that. 'Maybe
we could...' She paused as his phone rang, waited while
he took the call.

'Sorry about that.' His expression was grim when he
came off the phone. 'Right, I'll see you in the morning.
We start at six.'

'Sure.' Ella took a deep breath. 'I might get something to eat in the restaurant, if they're still taking orders.'

'Of course they are,' Santo said. 'I told them we
would not be finished filming till late. They are being
very good—they understand the odd hours.' His phone
bleeped again, and his teeth gritted. 'Enjoy your dinner.' He dismissed her and, now she had said where
she was going, Ella had no choice but to head into the
restaurant. She told herself she was a working woman
and there was nothing to be embarrassed about asking
for a table for one, but all she felt was awkward. There
was Vince, but he was engrossed in conversation with
another of the actors and it was clear there was some
serious flirting going on. Just when Ella had ordered,
just when she had decided it wasn't so bad after all, in
walked Santo, still talking on his phone. She smiled as
he walked towards her, but the smile disappeared when
he returned it and then promptly walked past her.

Ella couldn't believe he'd take things that literally,
would have them sit alone rather than share a meal, but
as Marianna came in, Ella realised that Santo had no
intention to eat alone.

It was work, Ella told herself as she twisted pasta

around her fork and tried not to hear their talk and laughter. It was exactly the same as she and Santo had done, in many hotels on many occasions, she told herself.

But did it take a bottle of wine to go through his diary?

It really was a hell of her own making, Ella told herself over and over through the coming days.

On a shoot it was a small closed world, but not even that could filter out the whispers and rumours that abounded about the Correttis. Ella watched as Santo read a newspaper, one that announced that the cousins were firmly divided, that Carlo's children were having nothing to do with Benito's, and that they were going to offer a counterproposal against Santo's half-brother, Angelo, who had the full weight of Battaglia behind him. Ella knew it must be killing him, knew the effect that it would be having on Teresa too.

Yet, unless it was relevant to the movie, Santo gave her not so much as a word as to what was going on in his life.

His usually smiling face was closed now, his eyes constantly hidden behind dark glasses, but Ella could see the tension in his lips, could hear the impatience in his words as he endlessly spoke on the phone. She loathed that at one point, as they were discussing the next scene, Marianna came over and asked if she could have a word with him.

'In private...' Marianna said and then switched to Italian. *'Familia.'*

Ella watched as Marianna drew him aside, watched as Santo's features paled and his fingers moved to his neck, pulling at the top he was wearing as he did when rarely he was anxious. Then he reached for his phone.

'Is everything okay?' she asked at the first opportunity. They were back at the hotel and heading up to their rooms, but instead of pressing the button for her room, Ella tried to speak with him.

'Of course,' Santo said. 'It went well today. The whole crew seems happier.'

'I meant...' She took a deep breath. 'With you? Have you heard from Alessandro?'

'Ella, I thought we agreed that we were talking only about work.'

'Santo, I know that something's wrong.'

'And?' He glared. 'As I said, you can't pick and choose what bits of me you have. You want professional, then here I am. You are the one who said we can't be both. Now, did you want to speak about the movie?'

'No.'

'Then if you'll excuse me, I am going to get ready to go to dinner.' The lift was at his floor and Santo stepped out, but Ella followed him.

'Santo, please,' Ella said. 'I made a mistake. I thought if we just concentrated on work till after shooting, then it would be better for the movie.'

'And now you've changed your mind?'

'Yes.'

'And will you change it again tomorrow?' Santo said nastily. 'Will you go back on your sex strike, because this is not a nice game, Ella.'

'I'm not trying to play games.'

'I have done everything you ask of me. I have never pushed you to do anything that you don't want to do,

but you signed out of this, Ella. I know things have been
bad for you, but right now things are bad for me. That's
fine, I'll wear it. I can deal with tough times—though
it could have been a hell of a lot better with your support. But you were the one who chose separate rooms
and not to be there. So now, if you will excuse me, I
would like some dinner.'

'Can I join you then?'

'I already have company tonight,' Santo said.

'Marianna?'

'Of course.' He shrugged. 'I have more to sort out
than just this film at the moment.' And she was determined not to go there, to just say nothing, but the words
blazed from her eyes and, without hesitation, Santo answered them.

'What?' He wasn't Sicilian for nothing. His words
were harsh and direct. 'Is she too good-looking for me
to eat with?' Santo demanded. 'If I hire only ugly people will you trust me then?' He looked at her for a long
time. 'You know, I don't think you ever will.'

'Do you blame me?' She just stood there. 'I've seen
you in action, I know better than anyone....'

'No.' He walked right up to her face. 'Don't try to
turn this on me. The fact that you will never trust me
has nothing to do with me or my reputation, because
you haven't even given us a chance, not one. The fact is
you don't want to trust.' Santo said. 'We could be stuck
on a desert island and there would still be a problem.'

He could see tears in her eyes and the burn on her
cheeks as his words hit home, because he was right. It
wasn't Santo with some irredeemable past that was halt-
ing her. Ella didn't actually know if she was capable of

a full-blown relationship, did not know how to love and be fully, properly, completely loved back.

'You deny us even a chance.'

'No.'

'Yes,' Santo said. 'You made it very clear right from the start that you wanted no relationship with me. You set the tone, so don't blame me for meeting it. Don't blame me for respecting the distance that you insisted upon.' He raised his finger, to make a point in the way that every Italian man did. He watched her flinch, watched her head snap to the left, and his breathing came harder. 'So,' he said. 'You think now that I would hit you?'

'No.'

'Yes.' He shook his head in disgust. 'I will not take the blame for him—I will not take the shame for him. You are as trapped as your mother,' Santo said. 'You might be on the other side of the world to him, but really, you have never left home.'

Santo could not have been more insulted.

'I go now and eat with a grown-up.'

CHAPTER TWELVE

Santo was right.

Sort of.

Ella lay on her bed and rather than denying his words, rather than defending herself to herself, instead she saw the hurt in his eyes, the absolute offence taken by Santo, and she didn't blame him a bit.

It wasn't that she didn't want to trust him, more that Ella simply didn't know how to, had found it far safer to hide behind her career and excuses rather than take a chance with a relationship.

It didn't feel such a safe place now. It felt empty, and worse, it felt selfish. Ella knew that she hadn't been there for Santo, hadn't shared in the tough times with him, and because of that, she might have blown their slim chance.

Why the hell had she had to go and fall in love with Santo though? Of all the billions of people on the globe, how had someone with major trust issues ended up with a man as wickedly bad as Santo? Ella even gave a wry smile to the heavens at the cruel lesson they had sent her, but then jumped when her phone rang. Now she wasn't Santo's PA, it was unusually quiet, but she jolted again when she heard who it was.

'Mum?' It was the first time her mother had rung her since she had started off on her travels. 'Is everything okay?'

'Everything is fine,' Gabriella said. 'Well, the same,' she corrected. 'But I waited till your father was asleep so that I could speak to you.'

'Has something happened?'

'I miss you,' Gabriella said. 'It seems strange to know that you are there. What have you been doing?'

And Ella told her—not about the promotion, more the news her mother would be stunned to hear.

'You ate dinner with Teresa Corretti? Ella, you must be careful.' She sounded terrified. 'Do not tell your aunts.'

'Mum, she's a lovely lady and I don't think their name is all bad now. All the locals are watching the filming and seem really excited—'

'What did you eat?' Gabriella interrupted and it was actually a nice conversation. She told her about the food, and yes, her mother asked about the furniture. 'She gave me some olive oil to send you.'

'She gave you that for me?'

'She said you would miss it.'

'I do.'

There was a very long silence and then Gabriella revealed the real reason she had rung.

'Ella, I am so sorry.'

'Mum...' She was about to tell her to stop, but wasn't that what she scorned her mother for, for not talking about things, for just closing off?

'I should never have asked you to cover up for him, but I was scared. If we told the police, what would happen afterwards? You were right to get away and you are right to not want to speak with him. I will never ask you to again.'

'Thank you.'

How she'd needed to hear her mother say sorry and they spoke some more, cried some more. As Ella hung up on her mother, she knew that there was someone she had to say sorry to herself.

Properly though.

Except he was at dinner, and it really would be poor form to disturb, so Ella texted instead, asked if she could speak with him, that it didn't matter what time.

Ella wasn't surprised when he didn't answer.

She'd hurt him, offended him, and she knew that Santo was incredibly proud.

CHAPTER THIRTEEN

HE WAS SCOWLING and completely unapproachable on set the next morning, arms crossed. He was talking with Luca, one of his cousins, and the conversation didn't look as if it was pretty, but Ella tried to focus on Taylor.

'We're going to zoom in to a close-up,' Ella said to Taylor. 'Just go for it, but anything we can't get today, we'll get in the studio. I'm not going to be asking you to do this over and over. Just give it all you've got now.'

As Taylor headed off for a touch-up of hair and make-up, she glanced over to the dark brooding shadow of Santo. Luca was nowhere to be seen now. The cameras were all set up and ready and, even if she was dreading it, even if this might prove the most embarrassing moment of her life, still she had to face him—had to tell Santo that it wasn't a game she'd been playing, that she'd just not been able to stick to a playboy's rules.

She walked over to him, and even with dark glasses on, she could feel his eyes telling her to back off. He was leaning on a trailer, arms folded, and he said nothing as she walked over.

'I'm sorry.' God, it was a very hard thing to say when you absolutely meant it. 'I am so sorry. I know how much I insulted you yesterday. I know that you would never hit me.'

Still he said nothing. It was like talking to a cardboard cut-out of him because his face never moved, his body was still. The effusive, expressive Santo was lost to her now and she wanted him back.

'I spoke to my mum last night and I realised you are right. I have been holding back.' Ella took a deep breath. 'I've liked you for a very long time,' she admitted. 'A lot, and yes, I was jealous even if I didn't want to admit that I was. And because I know that you don't do long-term, I knew that by sleeping with you I'd be pretty much writing my own resignation. I knew that I wouldn't be able to work alongside you if you were with someone else.' She wished he would speak but, when he did, she wished that he hadn't.

'You assume so much.'

Santo looked at her from behind his dark glasses. Not once had she even hinted that his lifestyle bothered her—irritated her, maybe. He had heard the barbs. He thought of the cards he had had her dictate to the florist. Except there had been none in recent months, for the familiar, well-used lines had stopped coming so readily. Jewellery was a far easier option with a quick, simple line about matching her eyes…

And Ella had written them.

'It was a lot more than sex to me and I didn't want you to know how I felt, but now you do.'

'Taylor's taking her place.'

'Santo…'

'Get to work, Ella.'

She was shaking as she walked away from him. She

had told him everything and he had given her nothing back.

Not everything.

Ella knew she hadn't been completely open with him—but how? She wasn't about to play the sympathy card. She'd declined the chance to talk to him on too many occasions. It wasn't exactly fair to demand that right back now.

'Ready?' Ella checked in with her leading lady.

'You want to take my place?' Taylor asked when she saw Ella's brimming eyes.

'Right now, I probably could,' Ella admitted, 'except it wouldn't be acting.'

'If I get this right you can buy me a drink tonight,' Taylor offered. 'And I'll lend you an ear.'

Taylor did get it right.

Whatever place Taylor took her head to, she was in agony and it was a privilege to watch. To witness her pure pain. There was no question that Vince would be drawn to her. Absolutely the viewer would understand why the characters would make love on the beach a few minutes later. Ella almost wanted to tell Taylor to stop, to breathe, because even though Taylor was hardly making a noise, it was clear she was broken.

Her eyes were screwed closed against tears that squeezed out, her lips were pressed tight and there was this river of pain building. She was locked in hell, just as Santo had been that morning where she had found him crying in the bath.

It hit her then.

She remembered the tears that Santo had shed that morning, the hell he had been in, all they had shared. It had been, she was sure now, far more than sex for him too, and she'd just walked away from him.

The one time Santo had needed another, had been himself with another, she'd closed off.

Frantic, she looked away from Taylor for a second, and over to Santo, but he just stood there, his arms folded, watching the action, watching Taylor, as she now must.

Taylor's blue eyes were open. She was choking in tears. Then, even though they already had the shots, she repeated it just in case, turned her head to Vince, blanched as if she expected criticism and then her face moved in for his kiss. And what a kiss it would be, because now Ella knew for sure that this movie would work.

'Cut.'

The second Ella said it Taylor burst out laughing, from the high and the elation of a perfect scene.

'That was amazing!' Ella enthused. 'Just brilliant.' And she told Taylor the same again later when she bought her a drink, shy to be sitting and talking with someone as famous as Taylor Carmichael.

'You'd better get used to it,' Taylor said when Ella admitted how nervous she was to be talking to her off set. 'If this film does well, you're going to be known soon. You'll have scripts arriving…'

'I haven't really thought about after,' Ella admitted. 'I'm just trying to concentrate on getting this right. I know there won't be an opportunity like this again.' Her voice trailed off for a moment. 'I've been so focused on work I've forgotten what's important.'

'We all do it at times,' Taylor said. 'Santo will understand that.' Ella burnt red that what was going on was so obvious to everyone, but then it turned to guilt as Taylor continued. 'But things are pretty hellish for the Correttis at the moment.' She was direct without being indiscreet and Ella caught her eye. Taylor would know only too well what was going on at the moment, that compromising photo that surprisingly hadn't contained Santo had still had the scandal of the Corretti name attached to it! 'Maybe it's time to forget about work for a while,' Taylor suggested.

It was.

Ella finished up her drink and thanked Taylor again for her amazing work today and then headed to the lift, not to the safety of her room, but the danger of his, for she wanted to say sorry again. She wanted to explain, and properly this time, why she had flinched when he had raised his hand. And it had nothing to do with playing the sympathy card. It was about telling the truth and admitting just why she hadn't felt able to give them a proper chance. Ella took a deep breath and knocked on his suite door.

Silence, and then as she knocked again, it opened to her dread—the stunning Marianna, dressed in a hotel bathrobe, her lacy bra on clear show. She barely blinked when she saw that it was Ella.

'Scusi,' she said. 'I thought you were room service.' She gave a smile. 'Santo is just in the shower.'

And Ella said nothing.

'Ah, here it is now...' Marianna said as a large ice bucket and bottle of champagne was delivered to the room and a large table of food was wheeled in. All covered, of course, but Ella could guess as to what lay beneath and it didn't take much guesswork to know what she was interrupting.

'By the bed,' Marianna ordered.

Just as Santo liked it.

'Did you need him for anything in particular?'

'Nothing that won't keep,' Ella said and walked more than a little numb back to her room, waiting for the pain to hit, waiting, as she secretly always had been, to find out how it felt to have a heart broken by Santo.

CHAPTER FOURTEEN

ELLA WAS ON set at six, still numb, still waiting for the damn to burst as she braced herself to see a postcoital Santo, knowing that she had to somehow remain professional and not make any reference to what had happened between the sheets.

As she'd insisted on.

'Dove Santo?'

It was the word on everyone's lips and in the end Ella rang him, but it went straight to voice mail. So she rang the hotel and asked to be put through to his room, determined to keep the bitterness out of her voice if Marianna answered.

She didn't.

Signor Corretti, it would seem, had checked out.

'Marianna Tonito?' Ella enquired.

She had checked out too.

And then her phone bleeped a text from him.

Something important came up. Know the film will be okay in your hands. Marianna has left my diary for you. I know you have a lot to deal with, but can you make sure there is champagne for after-party?

Er, no, Ella corrected herself. This was how it felt like to have a heart broken by Santo, except the numb feeling remained. The sky didn't fall in, the damn didn't burst and Ella found out, to her infinite surprise, that she was actually incredibly strong.

'Something came up...' Ella told the assembled set. 'I've no idea when he'll be back but we're going to just carry on without Santo.' And so, too, must she. 'We'll be fine.'

Because he gave them no choice but to be fine.

Was nothing at all important to him?

'Come on.' Ella looked at her watch. They'd wasted enough time this morning already and she was not throwing her career and the career of others away over a man, even one as drop-dead gorgeous as Santo. Yes, Ella found out she could put a broken heart on hold, because, over the next few days there were plenty of dramas, tears and tantrums, just none from Ella. She dealt with them all. She had no choice but to—there was a ship coming in and three hundred extras and she dealt with all that too. And yes, she even ordered the champagne.

'Last day of shooting tomorrow,' Ella told everyone. 'I want us all here at four.'

The town was buzzing. The restaurants were open for all the extras. There was just such a high all around and Ella did her best to match it, just could not give in yet. She took a picture of the busy streets and one of the ship and thought of sending them to her mother, thought of ringing her tonight. She so badly wanted to know more about the dangerous Corretti men and the women who loved them, but Ella knew it might hurt a little more than she could bear right now, that she had to make this through without tears. She would have, Ella was sure of it, had there not been a certain some-one waiting for her back at the hotel.

CHAPTER FIFTEEN

'TERESA CORRETTI IS here,' the desk told her, clearly anxious that someone so revered had arrived unannounced. 'I explained that Santo was not here, but she has waited to speak with you.'

'Thank you.'

Ella looked over and, sure enough, there was Teresa. Ella forced a smile. 'I'm sorry, Santo isn't here....'

'I was aware of that.' Teresa kissed her on both cheeks. 'I came to see you.'

'Oh.'

'Come, we go through...I believe there is a nice bar lounge.'

Ella was more than a little taken back, and perhaps so, too, were the bar lounge staff. A woman dressed in black was a rare sight in here, and that it was the Corretti matriarch made it double so.

Teresa ordered them both a drink and made polite chatter as they waited for them to arrive, asking after her mother and if she had told her about her visit.

'I did.' Ella smiled. 'She didn't even pretend not to be fascinated.'

'How is the filming going?'

'Very well.' Ella struggled to keep the edge from her

voice as their drinks were served. It wasn't Teresa's fault that her grandson had walked off mid-shoot.

"You are the first woman Santo has brought to visit.' Ella fought with the blush that was spreading on her cheeks, not sure how to tell this elegant woman that she had already been royally dumped.

'Actually...' Ella was supremely uncomfortable. 'It's really not that serious between Santo and me.'

'Really?' Teresa frowned. 'I thought there was a lot of affection between the two of you.'

Ella could feel her grip tighten on the glass in her hand. Really, she couldn't say to this elderly lady that her grandson was an exceptionally affectionate man, with many.

'My grandson is very complicated,' Teresa said. 'Of all my grandchildren he is the one that...' She gave a helpless gesture. 'Even as a child he smiled and laughed, was the happy one, but his heart was black and closed.'

'Santo?' Ella checked.

'Santo.' Teresa nodded. 'He is the same now. He laughs, he is wild, but he lets no one close. Always there are women, yet you are the only one he has brought to see me.'

'Signora Corretti.' She just didn't know how to handle this. 'I don't think Santo was introducing us. I mean, I don't think he was bringing me to visit you in the old-fashioned sense.' She just couldn't do this any more. 'I think things are over between Santo and me.'

'You think?'

And she thought of Marianna, and how he could just up and leave. Even if Ella had somehow engineered it, manifested it almost, for she had offered him on a plate

such an irresistible temptation, it killed he had so readily taken the bait.

'I know,' Ella said. 'There are some things you just
can't forgive.' And she wasn't going to discuss his sex
life with his nonna, but when you loved a man like
Santo there were so many other reasons to be cross.
'He was supposed to care about this film. It was the
most important thing to him, to this village, to the family name. But without a second thought he just walked
off....' Then Ella begged, more for herself than the
movie, but it saved a little face. 'Do you know where
he is?' she demanded, 'What suddenly came up?' She
was starting to cry and didn't want to. 'Who he's with?'

'These are not questions that we ask in my family.'

No, they were so bloody corrupt, so powerful, they
made their own rules and didn't care who they mowed
over in the process.

'It's a movie...' Teresa shrugged. 'You can forgive
if you want to.'

'Maybe you can.' She looked at the older woman,
who she actually adored, which was why she could be
honest, rather than rude. Both knew they weren't talking movies. 'I never could.'

And it was a nice thing to know, to know she had
boundaries, that no matter how much she might love
him, that she wouldn't simply turn a blind eye. That
knowledge was enough to halt Ella's tears, to smile and
chat some more with Teresa.

To know she would get on with her life.

'I have to get back,' Teresa said a long while later,
when Ella was drooping and doing her best not to show
it. 'Or we could have a coffee...'

Ella went to shake her head, but though she might not be like her mother, she had been brought up to abide certain rules.

'That would be lovely.'

'Perhaps—' Teresa smiled '—we have an amaro... good for digestion.'

She had to be up long before the dawn but Ella obliged, joining Teresa in sipping the herbal syrupy drink, listening as she reminisced about Salvatore. 'I talk too much,' Teresa apologised.

'It's been lovely to talk,' Ella said.

'You are a good girl,' Teresa said as they walked out to the hotel where her driver was patiently waiting. 'You looked after me well tonight. It has been nice to be out.'

'I've enjoyed it too.'

She had, Ella realised, even if she was beyond exhausted, finding only the time to set her alarm before falling into bed, too zonked to think about Santo, too exhausted to think about the movie they would be wrapping up tomorrow.

CHAPTER SIXTEEN

SHE WOKE UP missing him though.

The final day of filming and Ella looked out from her hotel window. A stunning moon glittered off the water. She looked at the ship Santo had been so pedantic about and he hadn't even hung around to see it.

No, this was how it felt to have a heart broken by Santo. She was starting to feel it now, not just the hurt but the little flare of anger towards herself for her handling of things. But she plunged her heart back into deep storage and dressed in her favourite denim skirt and halter top and then deliberately, as if serving herself a warning, applied some mascara and not the waterproof kind either.

She could cry it all off tonight when it was over, could take a bottle of his blasted champagne that she'd ordered up to her room and drink it warm if she so chose.

She so didn't want ice.

It was the promise of that that got her through, because watching the final scene, with the ship behind them, watching the returning husband's hands roam Taylor's body and remembering Santo's hands doing the same to hers, had her biting on her lip, willing the scene to be over, for this day to be over so she could say she had made it through filming.

Oh, there would be some studio stuff, but the bulk of it was done, or it would be a few seconds from now.

She watched husband and wife kiss, and as his hands explored her body, the infidelity was revealed. The whole set was in tears, even Ella. The ocean was just glimmering the ship, the extras all in harmony, and as the camera zoomed further in, Ella looked through her viewfinder. It could not be more perfect until she felt someone standing beside her, knew without turning her head that Santo had returned. And it could not be less perfect now because Santo was by her side and so badly she wanted him, despite everything, still she did and Ella was determined not to look around.

'Call cut.'

'Not yet.'

'Please,' Santo said, 'then I can take you back to the trailer.'

He had to be joking.

'I need to speak with you.'

'I'm kind of busy right now....'

But she called cut, because it was over, and there were cheers and applause from the crew as they wrapped up. Ella wiped her eyes with a tissue, saw the black streaks and let out a wry laugh. For all her effort not to cry over him, now she had to face him looking like a panda.

'Those tears aren't for you.'

'I know,' Santo said. 'I was watching you.'

She wished he wouldn't. Ella tried to keep her mind

on work—she couldn't bring herself to look at him. 'It's all gone well. I need to go and congratulate—'

'Not right now. I need you to come with me.'

She turned and looked and it was like the first morning she had slept with him. His left eye was black, and there was a small cut above his lip, but this time she absolutely did not want to know the details. She wanted as far out of Santo's personal life as possible.

'There is something I need to tell you,' Santo said, 'something you may feel…' His usually excellent English faltered. 'You may feel that I have overstepped the mark.'

Ella closed her eyes. Really, she had thought it something she could never forgive, and yet, in some masochistic streak, she had ensured Santo had his perfect choice of woman working for him, while she had sulked and hidden. Now she had to pay the price for dangling temptation in front of so readily tempted eyes. She had made a stupid move in a very grown-up game with a very liberal man, and now she couldn't really stand here and protest that he had taken the bait.

No, this wasn't a conversation they could have here. They were being handed glasses of champagne and the party was starting. Ella followed him to his trailer, dreading this conversation, but preparing herself to face it.

'I never really intended for it to happen,' Santo said. 'It was an impulse thing.…'

And she tried to play the grown-up game, to shrug it off, to say she understood, except tears were welling in Ella's eyes and there was a burn in her gut. No, she couldn't do it.

'If a man deceives me once, shame on him. If he deceives me twice, shame on me.'

She said the old Italian proverb that Santo must know off by heart, for it had been surely cussed to him many times. On this occasion he did not correct her Italian, and Ella spoke on. 'You know, everything I love about you is the part I hate too.'

He frowned.

'I'm not going to forgive you.' It was who she was. 'I know that sounds really unsophisticated, but maybe that's who I am. I can't forgive....' She closed her eyes, because she had withdrawn so rapidly that she had practically hand-passed him to someone else. 'I never expected you to take this as seriously as me.'

'Oh, I take this very seriously.'

'I know about Marianna.'

'Marianna?' Santo frowned. 'Marianna's gone.'

'Of course she is, because she slept with you.' He had to see her point. 'That's why I can't mix the two.'

'Ella, I think it is crazy that we do not sleep together. It has been driving me crazy, but I respect it. But Marianna...' He shook his head. 'Do you really think I took it all so lightly?' His hands moved in exasperation. 'I had to fire her, she came on to me.' He looked at her nonplussed face. 'I came out of the shower and...' He gave a tight shrug. 'You do not need detail but there was champagne and too much lace and suggestion...' He gave her the smile that melted, the smile that could well shoot her straight back to his bed. 'Nothing happened—we did not even kiss.' He gave a small yikes look. 'I fear I have lost my prowess unless she comes with much baggage and is more focused on camera angles than me.'

'You didn't sleep with Marianna....'

'I told you not.' Santo never lied. Ella realised it then. Never once did he try to cover up his mistakes. 'She tried, but I could not even be bothered to. Not even a stirring...' He actually seemed to think about it for a moment. 'Maybe a teeny one...' He held his thumb and forefinger up. He was just so honest Ella actually smiled and that was all it took for him to move straight in for the kill. 'I've missed you so much.' He pulled her into him, buried his head in her hair. 'I want you so much.'

'Santo—' she struggled '—you can't just disappear and then come back as if nothing's happened.'

'I can...' He was at her top, undoing the straps, just so impatient. 'You'll forgive me soon, but first I have to have you.'

'No.'

'I have to...' he moaned. He was peeling off her top now. 'Ella, please, it's been too long.'

'Where the hell have you been?' She looked at his battered face. 'Santo?'

'You don't need to know now.'

'I do,' Ella begged. 'I need to know what's been going on. I'm sorry I shut you out. I'm sorry I wasn't there for you while you've been having problems. I was so locked into me, into looking out for me, that I forgot all you're going through.'

'And...' Santo pushed her to go on, unhooking her bra as he did so and burying his face in her breasts.

'I was wrong,' Ella admitted.

'Why?'

He sucked her nipple. 'Why?' he growled.

'Because...' she flailed.

'Because I need you to be there for me,' Santo said. He took down her skirt and pushed her onto the bed and then undressed himself with Santo haste. 'The same way I need to be there for you.'

'Where have you been, Santo?'

He was kissing her all over and then he paused.

'Can I tell you after?'

She lay there squirming and not just with indecision. 'Do you really have to know now?'

And she looked up at him, looked at the want and the passion that needed matching, not questions and answers.

'No.'

'Say it again.'

'No.'

'No what?'

'No, right now I don't need to know where you've been.'

'Because?' He parted her legs, and she lay there naked and beneath him. And just like their first time it was Santo completely in control. He dragged out of her the truth, her answer, one she didn't know till now. 'Are you turning a blind eye, Ella?' Santo asked.

'No.'

'Which means?'

Yes, what did it mean? Ella asked herself. If she didn't need to know where he'd been, if she didn't require immediate explanation... 'That I trust you.'

And surely he should reward her with his naked

length, but he was a bastard, a good one though, because he made her wait, made her say it first.

'Which means?' Santo demanded.

'That I love you.'

'Right answer,' and she got her reward then. She loved him—she'd always known it, had just held back on it. It actually didn't matter in that moment if he loved her or not too, because it didn't change things, and she learned more in those blissful moments than she could learn in lifetime.

She loved him, like it or not, returned or not, quite simply she did. Ella stopped fighting it then, just gave into the bliss of being back in his arms as he took her to a place that only Santo could.

After, she covered herself with a sheet, as she always did, Santo noted, and he turned to her. 'You love me?' He grinned.

'Fool that I am.'

'I am very lovable.'

'So your nonna told me.'

Santo laughed, but it faded as she squealed when, mortified, Ella dived under the sheets as the trailer door opened.

'I didn't see a thing,' came a vaguely familiar voice, one that sounded not in the least embarrassed at what he had found. 'I'll come back....' She was just burning with shame beneath the sheets. 'I was told the interview—'

'Paulo?' She heard Santo speak, could not believe he was prolonging the agony. 'How soon can you start?'

'Is "now" the right answer?'

Clearly it was, though Ella thought she might die as the conversation continued. Did Santo have to be quite so comfortable with sex? But then again, Ella realised, Santo's PAs saw an awful lot, so Paulo might just as well get used to it.

'I need you to sort out a selection of rings,' she heard Santo say. 'Engagement rings,' he clarified as her heart stood still.

'Is there anything in particular you have in mind?'

'Her eyes are amber,' Santo said, 'but she would think that I was being superficial—'

'As well as cheap,' Paulo said.

'I know.' And she listened as Santo pretended he had come up with an idea, as if he hadn't planned every second of this. He was a step ahead of her all of the time. 'A diamond,' Santo said, 'as big as an ice cube, the shape of an ice cube....'

'Princess cut,' Paulo said. 'Leave it with me.' From beneath the sheet she heard Paulo move for the door. 'And don't worry, Ella,' Paulo called out, 'you don't have to take me out for dinner.'

'He seems good,' Santo said as he pulled back the sheet. 'And I can't see myself ever fancying him. Still...' He smiled. 'You know what they say—never say never.'

'You're incorrigible.'

'Only with words,' Santo said. 'And from now on, those words are only to you.' She looked up at him. 'I'm done,' he said. 'I'm through. I will have Paulo cancel my condom order from my shopping list and, if you will have me, I am exclusively yours.'

It wasn't the most romantic proposal but they were the nicest words she had ever heard.

'I will never hurt you,' Santo said.

'I know.'

She did.

'I mean it, Ella. I want to marry you as soon as Paulo can arrange.'

'We'll just slip away...' She couldn't believe they were actually discussing a wedding, their wedding.

'No.' Santo shook his head. 'We will do this properly. A good Sicilian wedding.'

'How!' Ella asked. 'We've no idea where your brother is, and my parents would never come.'

'Hey,' Santo broke in. 'I thought you said that you trusted me.'

And she remembered then how much she did. 'Teresa came and saw me.' Ella turned to him. 'She told me some of the stuff that's going on in your family. I'm sorry I haven't been there for you.'

'You're here now,' Santo said. 'And you can make up for lost time—believe me when I say that there is plenty more to come.'

'I'm sorry your family is such a mess.' She ran a finger over his bruises.

'So is yours,' Santo pointed out. 'Your father likes to use his fists....'

Ella didn't want to talk about that now and she went to tell him that, but Santo spoke first.

'I promise you though, I didn't hit him back.' He saw her eyes widen in realisation, an appalled look on her face as she realised that the bruises he wore came from her own stuffed-up family. 'I went to ask your father for permission to marry you and I saw firsthand how it was.'

'Santo!' She was panicking, appalled at what must have taken place, what her mother was going through at this very moment. As she went to rise from the bed, he grabbed her, pinned her down with his weight.

'Your mum's here,' Santo said. 'She is staying for a couple of nights with my nonna and then we will take her to meet with her sisters.'

It was too much to take in. 'She left.'

'She was scared to, but yes. She came back on the plane with me,' Santo said. 'You have to understand our ways. It is the same for my grandmother—they are loyal, their vows are more important than themselves.'

'How though?' Ella asked. 'She wouldn't leave for me. How did you convince her?'

'I spoke to my nonna.' He looked at Ella. 'I wanted to better understand...I wanted to know what best to say when I spoke to your mother.'

'How would she know?' Ella didn't get it. Yes, the two women were similar, both very locked in ways of old, but their lives were completely different. She looked to Santo and saw that for once he was struggling with words, not avoiding talking and not deflecting, just breaking a lifetime of silence. Ella knew how hard that could be.

'Salvatore beat her.' Santo's lips were white as he said it, curling in disgust at what his own blood had done.

'She told you?'

'Never.' Santo shook his head. 'That is one reason she liked you. You played by family rules. You say things are fine, you stay for dinner, you do what a good Sicilian girl should, but I have told her that that ends now. There will be no silence on certain subjects and my nonna agrees. She had held her secret for too long.'

'How did you know?'

'That birthday party she was talking about. I was listening at a door—I did a lot of that—and I heard my father confront him, said what he had seen all those years ago.'

'What did Salvatore say?'

'That is was just once.' Santo looked at her. 'That is no excuse.' Ella just lay there. 'No one else knows this, not even Benito, and I have told my nonna I will not repeat...except to you. It is her story to tell if she feels she needs to.'

'Why wouldn't he have told Benito?'

'To spare him perhaps?' Santo shrugged. 'They were rivals, but at the end of the day they were still brothers.'

She couldn't believe he would go and speak with his nonna, that he would confront so boldly a shame from the past, just to better help her, and she told him the same.

'Of course I would,' Santo said. 'I will always stand by you as in the coming months you will stand by me as my family tears itself to shreds.'

'They might not,' Ella said. 'There must be some bond there—you're related.'

'The worst enemies to have,' Santo said. 'Because they never go away. But at times they prove to be the best allies too. My nonna said that despite all he had done, your mother would be scared for your father too.'

'I'm scared for him,' Ella admitted, for though she loathed all he had done, the thought of him alone and suffering did not bring comfort when once she had thought that it would. 'I'm scared for him too.'

'You don't have to be,' Santo said. 'I have arranged a nurse daily, a housekeeper. He will be looked after, but not by your mother. I promised your mother all these things to get her to leave, and I did not hit your father back, but had I known what I do now, I might not have managed such restraint. I spoke at length with your mother. It is a long flight from Sydney to here.' He watched the colour spread across her cheeks and the tears pool and then fall from her eyes.

'He beat you.'

'Once.'

It was a pale defence of her parents and his expression struggled not to move.

'I left home as soon as I could and I got a place and enough money. Then a few months ago I went back to get her....'

'How badly did he beat you?'

And he insisted on details—he did not believe her mother's version, he only believed in her—and so she told him. She pulled back her head and showed him the scar and that capped expensive smile, and his face never moved a fraction. 'I should have gone to the police—pressed charges. But I knew that it would only make things worse for her. I just could not believe she would stay after what he did to me.'

'She does not think you can forgive her.'

'I'm trying to.'

'I will try then too,' Santo said. 'I will never show her my anger, but...' He swallowed it down. 'She's here now. I said that we needed tonight and we will go over tomorrow.'

'That's not very Sicilian.' Ella smiled.

'I know.' He grinned back, but then he was serious. 'You will work through it with your mother, I am sure.'

'We're already starting to. I almost rang her last night....'

'Why do you think you were sitting drinking in a bar with my nonna?'

She turned and grinned in quiet surprise.

'You sent her!'

'Of course! Surely you know that the Correttis are very good at arranging decoys. We were so worried you might ring home and get your father, so Teresa suggested we make sure that you were too tired to even think of ringing home.'

Santo climbed from the bed. 'And now,' he told her, 'we have an after-party to go to. I have been around long enough to disappear and be forgiven, but your career is still new.'

Even in that, he was looking out for her. Ella looked over to him, to the man she could not wait to marry, to the man she could not wait to spend the rest of her life with. His eyes met hers and they told her he loved her just the same. There was time for one more kiss before they headed out to the party and then Santo suddenly remembered something.

'I haven't told you I love you.'

'I think you just did.'

'Well, to be certain.' He pulled her back to his arms. 'I love you,' he said. 'And I have never said that to another. I love you so much that I will spend the rest of my life proving to you that, though you had every reason to be wary of me, you were so right to trust me.'

And Ella answered with a truth of her own. 'You already have.'

EPILOGUE

THE REFORMED SANTO didn't come wrapped in a bow.

But, as was the Sicilian way, there was a huge white bow on the church in her mother's village to show that there was a wedding about to take place.

'Even in my dreams,' Gabriella said as they walked along the dark cobbled streets lit by flaming torches towards the church, 'I never thought I would see this.'

'Where your daughter marries a Corretti?'

'I still cannot believe it!' Gabriella smiled. 'But no, that I would see you married in my church, with my sisters there....'

Together Santo and Paulo had worked wonders. Yes, they had wanted quick and discreet—the family was too fractured to make for a pleasing wedding and there was still a twist of pain for Ella when she thought of her father who, through his choices, would not be here for this day—but for Santo there were certain traditions that he would not cast aside.

Still, if it was her mother's dream wedding, it was going to be a small one. Teresa would be there, and her aunts, and she had two tiny nieces as flower girls, though it didn't matter to Ella. As the church doors opened, all she wanted to see was her groom.

'Oh!' The church was packed, all heads turning and smiling.

'Your soon-to-be husband has been sweet talking the locals. They are all happy to see me back and want to welcome, too, my daughter.'

And no doubt they were all delighted to have a Corretti just a little beholden to them, Ella thought as she walked towards her ex-reprobate and soon-to-be husband. He looked at her very pale green dress, which had once been her aunt's, and he smiled.

'I wondered how you would get around that!' Santo said as he greeted his bride, but in English, which the priest did not speak.

'It's for fertility,' Ella said, because in old Sicilian tradition, a green dress was sometimes worn and certain traditions worked best at times. They had known for all of three days that there was no trouble in the fertility department and they were brimming with excitement at their secret news.

It was the most wonderful service. He smiled as she made her vows in Italian. Santo was actually nervous for once as he made his, Ella knew, because his fingers moved to his neck as if to loosen his collar. But she knew when he gave them that they came from the heart.

And now they were married.

'We stay here,' Santo explained as they waited in a small house close to the church. 'Now they set up for the party.' He pulled her onto his knee. 'And we behave.'

'Of course.'

And he told her about the house he had seen in Palermo, but first they were going to go and lie on that beach as she should have done ages ago.

'But then I wouldn't have met you.'

The Sicilians did know how to throw a good party. The streets were lined with tables. There was food and more food, and speeches and then more food, but there was talking and laughter too. Ella looked over to her mother, chatting with Teresa, and she could never, even in her wildest, dreamt of this moment either.

'We dance now,' Santo said.

And she had thought the wedding would just be a formality, but being held in his arms, maybe Ella did have a few romantic bones in her body, for it was the best night of her life and she looked up at him and never wanted to change him.

'I love you.' She said it so easily now. 'Never change.'

'Only for good,' Santo answered in all seriousness. 'But not too good...' he added. 'I have chosen three scripts to take on our honeymoon.' Ella frowned as they danced their first dance. She really didn't want to talk about work.

'One, a hostage situation,' he whispered in her ear. 'There is a lot of dialogue, they talk a lot....' She was starting to smile.

'One, a romance,' Santo whispered. She smothered that smile in his chest, so grateful for the imagination that had saved her as a child, as she made a new movie in her mind. 'God, I love our work so much,' Santo said to her ear. 'We are never going to be bored.'

No, with Santo, you could never, ever be bored. 'And the third?' Ella asked, her stomach folding over on itself in want as she gazed up to him.

'A western.' Santo's face was deadpan as he looked

down to her, watched her start to laugh in his arms as to the visions that conjured up.

And happiness was infectious.

The party smiled and starting tapping spoons on their glasses for the lovely bride and groom to seal it with a kiss.

'It's tradition,' Santo said. 'You have no choice but to kiss me.'

No, no choice at all, but it was for more than tradition when her lips met his then.

It was simply for love.

* * * * *

*Read on for an exclusive interview
with Carol Marinelli!*

BEHIND THE SCENES
OF SICILY'S CORRETTI DYNASTY

It's such a huge world to create—an entire Sicilian dynasty. Did you discuss parts of it with the other writers?

There is generally a huge flurry of discussions at the start. Then we all seem to go off into our own worlds to write our own stories and come back for fine-tuning.

How does being part of the continuity differ from when you are writing your own stories?

My own stories are tiny seeds that I grow, but when I am a part of a continuity I am given flowered seedlings and lots of them. I am usually a bit of a hermit when I write—being in a continuity forces you not to be.

What was the biggest challenge? And what did you most enjoy about it?

One of my biggest challenges was writing an epilogue for a book that was first in a series with many secrets still to be revealed that I couldn't reveal. What did I enjoy? The moment when I worked out how to do it—I had so much fun researching, which can be a major procrastination tool, but when I found out that Sicilian brides used to wear green it all started to slot into place.

As you wrote your hero and heroine, was there anything about them that surprised you?

Their love of ice! More seriously, my hero really surprised me and, in turn, my heroine too. There was a pivotal scene at the beginning of the book that I struggled with and kept trying to dilute and, after a *lot* of rewriting and trying to change him, I ended up going back to my original vision of that scene.

What was your favourite part of creating the world of Sicily's most famous dynasty?

I love writing about complex family ties. A Sicilian dynasty was like a moth to flame for me—though I knew it would burn.

If you could have given your heroine one piece of advice before the opening pages of the book, what would it be?

I don't think I would have—people make their own mistakes and find their own happy endings.

What was your hero's biggest secret?

His whole life was a secret—and he was unearthing that fact.

What does your hero love most about your heroine?

He shares her imagination.

What does your heroine love most about your hero?

He shares her imagination, too.

ROMANCE

A Rich Man's Whim	Lynne Graham
A Price Worth Paying?	Trish Morey
A Touch of Notoriety	Carole Mortimer
The Secret Casella Baby	Cathy Williams
Maid for Montero	Kim Lawrence
Captive in his Castle	Chantelle Shaw
Heir to a Dark Inheritance	Maisey Yates
A Legacy of Secrets	Carol Marinelli
Her Deal with the Devil	Nicola Marsh
One More Sleepless Night	Lucy King
A Father for Her Triplets	Susan Meier
The Matchmaker's Happy Ending	Shirley Jump
Second Chance with the Rebel	Cara Colter
First Comes Baby...	Michelle Douglas
Anything but Vanilla...	Liz Fielding
It was Only a Kiss	Joss Wood
Return of the Rebel Doctor	Joanna Neil
One Baby Step at a Time	Meredith Webber

MEDICAL

NYC Angels: Flirting with Danger	Tina Beckett
NYC Angels: Tempting Nurse Scarlet	Wendy S. Marcus
One Life Changing Moment	Lucy Clark
P.S. You're a Daddy!	Dianne Drake

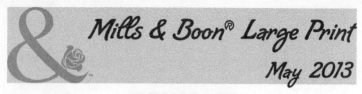

ROMANCE

Beholden to the Throne	Carol Marinelli
The Petrelli Heir	Kim Lawrence
Her Little White Lie	Maisey Yates
Her Shameful Secret	Susanna Carr
The Incorrigible Playboy	Emma Darcy
No Longer Forbidden?	Dani Collins
The Enigmatic Greek	Catherine George
The Heir's Proposal	Raye Morgan
The Soldier's Sweetheart	Soraya Lane
The Billionaire's Fair Lady	Barbara Wallace
A Bride for the Maverick Millionaire	Marion Lennox

HISTORICAL

Some Like to Shock	Carole Mortimer
Forbidden Jewel of India	Louise Allen
The Caged Countess	Joanna Fulford
Captive of the Border Lord	Blythe Gifford
Behind the Rake's Wicked Wager	Sarah Mallory

MEDICAL

Maybe This Christmas…?	Alison Roberts
A Doctor, A Fling & A Wedding Ring	Fiona McArthur
Dr Chandler's Sleeping Beauty	Melanie Milburne
Her Christmas Eve Diamond	Scarlet Wilson
Newborn Baby For Christmas	Fiona Lowe
The War Hero's Locked-Away Heart	Louisa George

Mills & Boon® Hardback

June 2013

ROMANCE

MEDICAL

Mills & Boon® Large Print

June 2013

ROMANCE

Sold to the Enemy — Sarah Morgan
Uncovering the Silveri Secret — Melanie Milburne
Bartering Her Innocence — Trish Morey
Dealing Her Final Card — Jennie Lucas
In the Heat of the Spotlight — Kate Hewitt
No More Sweet Surrender — Caitlin Crews
Pride After Her Fall — Lucy Ellis
Her Rocky Mountain Protector — Patricia Thayer
The Billionaire's Baby SOS — Susan Meier
Baby out of the Blue — Rebecca Winters
Ballroom to Bride and Groom — Kate Hardy

HISTORICAL

Never Trust a Rake — Annie Burrows
Dicing with the Dangerous Lord — Margaret McPhee
Haunted by the Earl's Touch — Ann Lethbridge
The Last de Burgh — Deborah Simmons
A Daring Liaison — Gail Ranstrom

MEDICAL

From Christmas to Eternity — Caroline Anderson
Her Little Spanish Secret — Laura Iding
Christmas with Dr Delicious — Sue MacKay
One Night That Changed Everything — Tina Beckett
Christmas Where She Belongs — Meredith Webber
His Bride in Paradise — Joanna Neil

0513 GEN STD LP